WII

Tom Burton

Dear Linda,

Hope you enjoy these stories —
had a lot of fun writing them!

J. Burton.

First published in Great Britain in 2020

Set in Garamond

ISBN: 979-8-55904-976-2

For April Duncan,
who planted the seeds of this book,
nurtured its first green shoots,
and helped these stories blossom.

Thank you.

CONTENTS

1
HORN AND HOOF

'. . . Why don'tcha grab it yet?'

'Hush now. I'm concentrating.'

'But I'm *hungry!*'

'Shush!' Flamefur nipped Dusksilver's ear as they crouched motionless in the swaying grass, watching the rabbit snuffle along the muddy path. It paused, twitched an ear and inched closer. Hunger prickled Dusksilver's belly like thorns as the wind hissed through the heather. Their prey crept closer.

Closer . . .

Closer . . .

The rabbit froze. Lifted its head. Sniffed the air.

And Flamefur pounced.

A flash of fiery lightning. A ragged snarl. A terrified shriek.

Flamefur crunched the life out of the rabbit, her jaws locked deep into its throat until its feeble twitches stopped. Dusksilver squirmed eagerly as her mother butchered the carcass until – finally! – Flamefur nudged the steaming liver towards her daughter. 'Go on,' she smiled. 'Dig in.'

Dusksilver gobbled it down, warmth flooded through her belly. Sated, she nuzzled against her mother. 'Thanks, Mum!'

Flamefur licked her brow. 'That'll teach you not to complain, won't it?' she chuckled.

A twig cracked. Flamefur raised her bloody muzzle as Dusksilver shrank against her, trembling. Something was crunching through the bracken towards them!

A huge beast melted out of the mist, towering over them. A mighty stag crowned with curving antlers, his back as broad as a bull's, his glossy coat shimmering with muscle and a great shaggy mane beneath a proud stern face.

Flamefur hunkered down into the earth. 'Bow your head,' she whispered in reverence. 'Show respect. The Moor Lord rules this land.' Dusksilver buried her muzzle into her forepaws, trembling. Hot breath washed over her face. She peeked up; dark wise eyes gazed back.

'And who might you be?' the stag rumbled, his deep voice tinged with amusement.

Dusksilver shrank into the ferns. 'I–I'm just a cub, sir,' she stammered.

2

A snort of laughter. 'No need to call me "sir", young 'un. Makes me feel old. Just call me Bruton.'

'Daaad! Wait up!' A lanky fawn wobbled into view on spindly legs, his tawny coat speckled with white. Tottering sideways, he collapsed into the ferns with a giggle.

Bruton huffed a weary sigh. 'Ronan, a Prince does *not* make such a fool of himself. He maintains dignity and walks with pride. We have guests.'

Ronan struggled upright. 'Sorry, father.' He stumbled forwards to brush noses with Dusksilver; she giggled as he licked her muzzle.

Bruton rolled his eyes. 'Aren't children *wonderful* when they're young?'

Flamefur snickered in commiseration. 'They certainly are, sir!'

Suddenly a distant wail sliced through the stillness. Bruton's head whipped around, ears pricked. Dusksilver shrank against her mother. A distant bark echoed; then another, and another. More and more voices joined in a terrible chorus, like a snarling pack of demons.

'The hunt!' Bruton roared. 'Stay hidden! I'll lead them off!' Flamefur and Dusksilver wormed beneath the prickly gorse bush, Ronan quivering beside them. The stag raised his head, bellowed in defiance and thundered away through the bracken.

3

They huddled together, breathless with dread. A spider crawled across Dusksilver's snout, but she dared not sneeze. The baying voices grew louder and louder until a ragged pack of hounds burst into view, plunging through the heather and baying with bloodlust. Pounding behind them came a huge dark horse with its rider in a blood-red coat, his wailing horn spurring the pack onward.

They passed by the hiding place, their terrible clamour fading on the wind.

Flamefur crawled out from beneath the bush. 'Stay here. I'll be right back.'

Dusksilver nuzzled against her. 'No, don't! Please, Mum!'

Her mother curled around her. 'Hush now. That stag led the pack away. I'm going to help him. Besides,' she tenderly licked Dusksilver's brow, 'someone's got to watch over this poor fawn until his father returns. Imagine how much safer he'll be knowing a brave cub like you's protecting him, eh?'

Dusksilver puffed out her chest proudly. 'Leave it to me, Mum. I won't let you down!'

Flamefur nibbled her ear. 'That's my girl!' Then she slunk away into the bracken.

Bruton pounded over the open moor, the baying hounds and rumbling hooves loud in his ears as he ran on. A screaming pheasant erupted out of the gorse and whirred up into the sky. Panting heavily, Bruton heard the hounds crashing through the heather behind him. He was a strong beast, but years of defending his kingdom had dulled his limbs and stiffened his bones, and the pack was fresh and eager. No chance of outpacing them over open ground.

High Falls! Of course – the twisting path guarded by a nest of brambles onto the high rocky spur overlooking the river, then into the beech wood and safety. Bruton galloped downhill into the jagged gully, brambles tearing at his coat as he forced his bulk out onto a wide promontory of rock. The frothing rapids thundered far below him, his coat jewelled with spray. A thicket of snagging brambles behind him, the treacherous slippery rocks underhoof – they wouldn't dare follow him. Surely!

A vicious snarl shattered the stillness; before Bruton could turn a huge shape crashed into him, fangs crunching deep into his hindleg. He bellowed and shook it off, but the hound scrabbled upright and lunged in. He stamped down desperately but it darted aside, claws raking his belly. With a mighty heave he wrenched free, backing against the cliff edge. Loose pebbles skittered down into the churning torrent far below. Blood speckled the rocks from a dozen ragged wounds.

Nowhere to run. Nowhere to hide. Gnawing agony ripped through him as he limped away from the cliff edge. The hound began to prowl. A black and tan mongrel with bristling hackles and dripping jaws, its eyes blazed with bloodlust as it circled him. It knew he was wounded and toyed with him, waiting to strike . . .

At least my son is safe. They'll never find him.

Bruton gritted his teeth and tossed back his head, his chin high in scornful defiance. *One good strike*, he thought, swishing his antlers. *One good crippling blow before he rips my throat out.*

The hound crouched, ready to spring. A low bubbling growl issued from its bared fangs. Bruton squared his shoulders and lowered his antlers, bracing himself for the final charge. With a savage howl the hound leapt—

A tawny blur smashed into the hound, bowling it sideways with a yelp.

Flamefur! She had crept up the shale-strewn slope and launched herself from above. They rolled over and over, clawing and snapping. Flamefur bit and bit again, quick as a striking viper, flank, snout and forepaw. But the hound clung on, fangs sunk deep into her brush as she twisted and writhed. Lashing out blindly she ripped one of its ears. It

6

howled and wriggled free. Flamefur scrambled upright as the hound flung itself upon her. She screamed as its jaws crunched into her shoulder—

A bellow of rage. Bruton's monstrous shadow loomed over them; before the hound could yelp the stag's antlers had swept it aside. Battered and whimpering it shrank back against the wall of rock.

Flamefur struggled to her feet, hackles bristling as Bruton stood tall beside her. Stag and vixen united as one against their common enemy.

The hound bared its teeth and howled, a final desperate killing lunge—

Bruton reared up, his hooves slamming into the hound mid-air. With a terrified scream it vanished over the cliff. Down. Down. Down into the churning white torrent.

Flamefur limped to the cliff edge, peering down into the hazy tumult. Nothing. Just the whispering trees and the rushing water far below.

Bruton slumped to the rocky floor with a groan. Flamefur trotted to his side, licking the ragged wounds across his belly.

Bruton gave a wheezing chuckle. 'Getting slow in my old age, huh?'

Flamefur licked his muzzle. 'Nonsense! Your son's waiting for you, c'mon!'

Bruton gritted his teeth and staggered up on

shaky legs. 'Onwards and upwards then, miss!'

Dusksilver huddled beneath the gorse bush, Ronan close beside her.

Heavy footfalls crunched through the bracken towards their hiding place. The horseman and his hounds! Ronan ducked his head, shivering with fright. Dusksilver bared her teeth, her hackles bristling . . .

'Dusky?' Flamefur called. 'Ronan? Come out! You're safe!'

'Mum!'

Dusksilver scrambled out from under the gorse bush, dancing with joy around her mother's legs. Bruton knelt gingerly into the bracken as Ronan nuzzled against his flank. 'You did it, Dad! You came back!'

Bruton smiled down at Dusksilver. 'And you kept him safe, hmmm? Brave little cub, aren't you?'

Dusksilver blushed as Flamefur licked her brow. 'She certainly is, sir!'

2
FOX FURY

Lexa hunkered down beside her mate. 'So you'll circle around and distract them from the north?'

Renn grinned. 'While you sneak in and steal the prize, sure.' Before them, the hillside sprawl of rocks echoed with excited chittering. The rank stink of stoat washed over them, spiced with the delicious scent of butchered rabbit.

Lexa wrinkled her nose. 'You sure about this?' Sharp-toothed, sinuous and bloodthirsty, a stoat gang was a formidable enemy.

Renn licked her cheek. 'We'll be fine. In 'n' out real quick, like always. Worked on Urthclaw, didn't it?'

Lexa snorted. 'He's a crotchety half-deaf badger as nimble as a legless pig. Bit different from this.'

They crept through the whispering grass towards the rocky outcrop of Cleave Tor. Across the moor, the steam train hooted as it thundered out of

Okehampton. A lark poured out its tinkling song from a gorse bush while Rorak the buzzard circled high on the thermals. He watched the foxes keenly, for their stealthy progress among the rocks meant rabbits. Under the morning dew the cobwebs glittered like diamonds, gossamer lace draped over the gorse. At the next boulder they parted ways, Lexa trotting uphill. 'Take care of yourself, Fart Face. No slip-ups, remember!'

Renn chuckled. 'You too, Dozy Paws.'

In the shadow of Cleave Tor, Chagga's gang swarmed around the dead rabbit. Chagga rested his forepaws on the carcass, fangs peeled back in a snarl.

'Will yew leave off!' he hissed. 'I eats first and when I've 'ad enough Ripnose can get stuck in. Yiss-yiss. Dat's fitch law.'

'But me 'n' Scratch caught dis thumper,' Shiv scowled. 'We oughta get first helping.'

'Mind yew don't get me fangs in yer throat, moss-muncher,' Chagga glared.

'There's four of us,' Shiv muttered.

'But it's yer throat I'll go for, me bucko. 'Sides, dis thumper's real plump. Would I cheat me own flesh 'n' blood?'

'Yiss,' Scratch sniggered. 'Yew'd eat granny if

she smelled like thumper. An' you wouldn't share 'er neither.'

Chagga bristled. 'Oh yiss? Anyone else wanna challenge me?'

'*I* will,' Renn growled. He had crept up behind the stoats to within easy pouncing distance. Chagga squeaked with fright. With a flurry of snakelike bodies his gang flowed down the nearest boltholes, lingering to hurl insults.

'Awful lot of rabbit for a small stoat,' Renn teased. 'Maybe you'd like to gift it to a better hunter.'

Chagga hunkered over the kill, baring the yellow thorns of his fangs. 'Try 'n' take it – sheep's scat!'

Renn grinned. 'Big talk for a scrounger – you as quick as your mouth?' He swaggered closer while Lexa stalked through the rocks behind, silent and unnoticed.

Chagga reared up proudly. 'Chagga ain't stupid. C'mon then, Canker Head!'

Renn darted in as Chagga rushed to meet him, hissing and spitting. Before they clashed the fox swerved aside and vanished into the shadows. Chagga turned and froze.

The rabbit carcass was gone!

'Filthy foxes!' he snarled. Climbing the granite summit he chakkered with rage, his harsh voice echoing about the jagged boulders as he summoned the stoats of Cleave Tor Tribe. High overhead, Rorak saw his lunch was lost and sailed away eastwards over the Taw river, mewling to his distant mate.

The gang rippled out of crannies and fissures to cluster below their leader.

'Bloody foxes!' Chagga hissed. 'We've bin robbed by stinkin' foxes. I hate 'em!' He turned on his tribe, seething. 'An' where woz yew, worm-brains? All o' yew stinkin' cowards scared of a mangy old fox!'

Shiv rose on his haunches. 'Dat Renn's fierce,' he piped up. ''E woz Oakpaw's pup, weren't 'e?'

Chagga spat contemptuously. 'So wot? Dat fleabag's pushin' up daisies now, ever since Man's wire got 'im. 'E ain't botherin' us no more!' His black eyes glittered. 'Five fitches could chop dat fox, easy. If Shiv 'n' Slickfang woz to come at 'is left side, an' Scratch 'n' Ripnose came at 'is right, then yours truly could rip out Canker Head's throat.'

Shiv shuddered. 'I ain't doin' nuffink. Dat Renn's a cunnin' fighter. Yer plan's gonna get us crunched like twigs, stupid!'

Chagga leapt upon the hapless stoat, bulling him over as he pricked Shiv mercilessly with his fangs.

'Wot d'yew want, idiot, me crown or yer head? 'Urry up 'n' speak!'

Shiv cowered among the broken grass stalks. 'Yaaargh, you's the chief!' he screeched. 'I only got one 'ead. Lemme live, please!'

Chagga rose, grinning as he eyed the other stoats. 'Wot're yew lot gawpin' at, eh? Anyone else wanna try?'

The others averted their gaze.

Down in the wooded valley the foxes skinned the rabbit, red meat warming their bellies as the Taw tinkled below them. A blackbird scolded them from a gnarled oak choked in moss. Chattering squirrels leapt across canyons of shadow, shivering the leaves high overhead.

Sated, Lexa snuggled into her mate with a contented sigh. 'Aaah, that's better. Your crafty plan worked, O clever-whiskers. I'm stuffed!'

Renn nipped her ear playfully. 'Glad to hear it, O pot-bellied pincher of conies. Left any for the cubs, did you, famine chops?'

Lexa giggled. 'Course I have, silly.' She wriggled free to dance around him, teasing. 'Can't catch me. Fart Face! Cabbage Breath!'

'Off with you, Dozy Paws,' Renn chuckled. 'See you back at the den.' They brushed noses, then

Lexa whisked away into the undergrowth with her tinkling laugh. Renn curled into the crinkled leaves, eyes drifting shut as a thrush sang him to sleep high above.

Lexa crested the hilltop and weaved through the twisted roots. She shuddered with eagerness at the prospect of home, the warm nuzzling welcome of her cubs as they squirmed over her with joyful squeaks.

She never saw the tripwire.

TWANG!

The snare hissed backwards and smashed her down into the earth. Cruel wire bit into her throat. Tighter. Tighter. The stink of fear broke from her coat as she gasped and writhed. She inched backwards, gulping ragged lungfuls of air as she twisted and jerked. Useless. Each frantic effort only brought a savage tug from the noose. The sun dimmed above her. Exhausted, she collapsed into the ferns with a wail of despair, misery prickling her guts. *My darling catkins, Meela and Suki. I've failed you.*

'Anything I can do, friendo?' chittered a shrill voice.

Chagga slunk into view, black eyes gleaming in triumph. 'Want me to loosen the wire with me teeth?'

Lexa bared her fangs proudly. 'Loosen my throat, more like.'

'Awww, don't old Mange Bag trust Chagga?' the stoat drawled. 'Ain't she grateful?'

'Don't play games with me, dungbrain.'

Chagga sniggered. 'Yew ain't in no position to be nasty, wiv no more foxes to back yew up. Heard yer ma's just worm-meat now. Miss 'er, do ya . . . Maggot Face?'

Lexa flung herself at the stoat but the snare yanked her back, leaving her choking in the grass.

'Yeeheehee!' Chagga chittered with glee. 'Snares suit ya – funnier than a thumper in a wire! Yew shouldn't'a crossed Chagga!' He rippled through the grass and sprawled before her. 'Listen, Fleabag. We ain't friends but I don't do the trapper's dirty work like them ferrets. What d'yew want me to do?'

'No tricks?' Lexa rasped.

'No tricks. I spit on all foxes, but Man is Man.'

Lexa sank onto her paws. 'There's a badger in the sett upriver. Greysnout. He and his sow could dig out the stake.'

'The brocks is great diggers 'n' miners, yiss-yiss,' Chagga agreed. 'I fetch him if yew promise one fing.'

'Name it.'

'No more coney-snatchin' off fitches. Never. Not ever.'

Lexa nodded.

'Don't go away, foxy-woxy,' Chagga grinned. 'Won't be long. Just hang in there, yeehee!' He rippled away, sniggering at his sick joke.

Weakened with exhaustion, Lexa slumped into the damp leaves. Her eyes drifted shut into slumber. High above the leaves were whispering.

A sharp jolt of pain ripped her back into wakefulness. Chagga had bitten her ear. Blood pulsed down her cheek onto her chestfur.

The stoat writhed around, helpless with laughter as his gang jeered at Lexa.

'Nice foxy collar!' Shiv sneered.

'Looks like a rat on the poacher's wall,' Slickfang crowed. Hissing sniggers dribbled out of the gloom, stoats flowing from boltholes to taunt the vixen gasping on the cold hard ground.

'Bet old Scat Stink thought I really woz gonna fetch ol' Brocky,' Chagga cackled. 'Imagine – nice bit o' hope to brighten 'er misery.' He narrowed his eyes. 'Never. Not ever! Chaggy went 'n' got 'is nearest 'n' dearest. Fitch can't gloat alone. Gotta share a good stoat gloat. Yik-yik-yik!'

Lexa gazed at her tormentor through pain-rimmed eyes. The cruel noose bit into her neck but she would never waste her breath on a slanging match.

Slickfang skittered forwards to crunch his teeth into her tail. Lexa yelped and twisted around, but Slickfang sprang safely out of reach. 'Blood Game! Yiss yiss!'

The others swarmed gleefully around her. 'Blood Game! Blood Game!' Each darted in to nip an ear or paw, or sink their teeth into Lexa's brush. 'Coo-ee . . . cooo-eee . . . Stoaties chew out foxy's liver, yiss-yiss . . . chomp-chomp! Stupid fox all alone in Stoatland . . . yew tasty, crow's guts!'

Tiny pointed teeth nipped the vixen's hindlegs; she was pricked all over by wicked fangs, her tail, her flank, her forepaws. Lexa swallowed the pain and gnawing grief. Bared her teeth. *I won't die cowering like a frightened rabbit*, she thought. *The hill fox clans will remember me.* Her hackles bristled and she growled in defiance.

'This 'un's got coney blood in 'er,' Ripnose sneered. 'I seen more fight in a blind mouse.' He hopped onto Lexa's back, his mocking voice washing over her. 'Behold, Mighty Fitch on the dungheap!'

Renn's savage roar sliced through the silence.

And death leapt down amongst them.

17

Lexa glimpsed the hurtling shadow half a heartbeat before she heard the shriek. Ripnose died first, blood gushing from his torn throat. Dimly Lexa saw him flung aside, knocking over two more. In a flash Renn was hunkered protectively over her, blood-blackened jaws agape in a howl of wild fury.

And threw himself into battle.

Lexa lay wide-eyed with shock, watching a dozen stoats take the most ferocious onslaught ever witnessed.

No fury more fierce was ever seen in the vicious world of beasts; where some desperate creature armed with teeth alone will spring upon a gang of scavengers looming over its fallen mate. The stoats scattered like roaches under the fox's vengeful charge, squealing in blind terror. Yet Renn was faster, stronger, and filled with roaring bloodlust as he smashed through the chittering gang.

Nowhere to run.

Nowhere to hide.

Slickfang turned to flee but Renn's jaws crunched through his ribs to hurl his broken body aside. He scythed through the stoats like a russet whirlwind, ripping and snapping as he ravaged the cowering pack. Renn, the fox who fought for his beloved Lexa. Renn, the one that fought with the raging fury of a great savage wolf.

Chagga twisted and screeched. His world somersaulted, pain smashing through a blur of bracken, rocks and sky. Heavy claws raked his belly and pinned him among the fallen leaves. Fetid breath blasted into his face. Once more he screamed for mercy, but jaws closed deep in his throat and silenced him forever.

The tattered remnants of Cleave Tor Tribe streaked into the undergrowth, wailing in defeat. Panting heavily, Renn lowered his bloody muzzle to gnaw stubbornly at the stake. Lexa whined as the noose bit into her throat.

The stake jolted loose. Wheezing and coughing Lexa squirmed free, shivering as Renn's teeth gently eased the wire over her head. She slumped into the trampled grass with an exhausted groan.

A cold damp nose nuzzled into her ear. Renn curled around her, thick tawny fur warming her weary bones as he licked her brow.

Lexa nuzzled into his chest. 'Better late than never, Fart Face,' she rasped with relief.

'Missed you too, Dozy Paws,' Renn grinned.

3
TOOTH AND CLAW

Mina the vixen loped through the icy woods, her pads crunching the frozen moss. A distant yip made her heart flutter. Cubs! Her heart sang with eagerness to return to her cosy earth, to the warm nuzzling welcome of Taka and Naveen.

The squeak echoed again. Prickled with curiosity, she zig-zagged through the slushy undergrowth to the ridge. A muddy clearing rimmed by towering pines, the mud churned up by the padding of many paws and littered with bone shards. A yawning black tunnel guarded by a huge jagged boulder at the foot of the slope.

She crept closer, sniffing the air. No doubt the cubs would be dozing in the den while the adults were out hunting.

Suddenly a huge grey beast slunk out from behind the boulder. Lean and shaggy, as big as a deer with gleaming golden eyes. Mina's breath froze: a wolf! Nightmare tales for her cubs, ravenous monsters of shadow and fang who devoured all prey they found. Sheep, cattle, even the baying hounds that ran her brothers down; wolves killed as they wished, and held no fear of Man. The wolf's scarred muzzle wrinkled into a snarl as it stalked towards her. Breathless, she edged back. The pack had left someone to guard the cubs. Stupid, stupid!

The cub-watcher advanced on her. Mina averted her gaze and whined in deference. 'Sorry! Don't attack!'

'Go away!' the cub-watcher growled. Slowly Mina withdrew to the far side of the clearing. At the tree-line she looked back. The cub-watcher was glaring after her, hackles raised, teeth bared. She shivered and trotted into the pines.

The chilly winter night descended as she trekked on. Frogs croaked in the reeds. An otter surfaced and stared after her. At the foot of a gnarled oak she stumbled upon a vole and crunched it down, the red meat warming her belly. In her mind she could already smell the musty tang of her earth, her mewling cubs clambering over her as she nose-nuzzled them to suckle. 'I'm coming home!' she yelped joyfully, and leapt over the twisted root.

The noose jerked around her neck and slammed her down into the frozen earth. *Snare!* She choked and writhed, her paws scrabbling for purchase as she struggled uselessly. The noose bit into her neck, dragging her down. Tighter. Tighter. She crawled back, gulping air as she whined. Her panic soaked the snow in a gush of stinking urine. The chilly night air was soiled with the fear seeping from her fur.

Think. Think! She had seen rabbits caught in Man's traps; their agonised hysteria only tightened the snare until they blacked out and died. She twisted and jerked. No use. Each effort only brought a savage clench from the noose, cruel cords cutting into her throat. The stars flickered and dimmed above her. Sucking in a desperate breath she wailed in despair.

A raven circled overhead, mocking her with its bubbling chuckle. Exhausted, she slumped into the frozen earth, sickened with dread. *My little ones*, her misery knotted her guts like thorns. *Taka and Naveen, I couldn't keep you safe.*

'Don't move.'

Bushes rustled. A hulking grey shadow melted out of the undergrowth. Mina chittered with fright: the wolf again!

But no. This one was broader, heavyset with age,

his shaggy fur glistening with silver. His snout unmarred by scars.

Mina shrank back, baring her teeth in a defiant snarl. 'Come to kill me, Scat-Stinker? I won't go quiet!' If she couldn't claw him, at least she could bite.

'The snare's fixed into that stump,' he rumbled. He tugged at the stake with his teeth, then padded closer to sniff at her. Mina twisted and bucked, the noose tightening around her throat.

'Keep still,' he growled. 'I can't help if you don't keep still.'

'What can you do?' she rasped. 'Kill me? Well, do it – do it!'

He snorted, sank onto his paws . . .

. . . and rolled onto his back. Baring his stomach and throat.

She stared, astonished. No hunter ever showed submission to a rival. It was Forest Law, stronger than blood or bone.

'My name's Torven. I'm *not* trying to hurt you,' the wolf rumbled. 'We ain't all as bad as you think.' He crawled closer, ears flattened. The universal sign for *Friend. Harmless.*

Mina edged backwards, whimpering as the noose bit into her throat.

The wolf snuffled close. 'Here. Let me.'

'How do I know you won't go for me throat?'

He snorted. 'What good'll that do me? I don't fight foxes.' His fangs gnawed at the rope. The snare loosened. A pause, then: 'Besides, no good meat on 'em. All sinew 'n' bone on you scroungers.'

She bared her teeth proudly. 'Maybe this scrounger'll rip yer ear off.'

'Maybe she will.' He chewed and tugged, voice muffled. But Mina could still hear the dry smirk in his tone. 'Maybe Miss Scrounger will sprout wings 'n' fly. Maybe she'll grow old 'n' grey 'n' ga-ga, just like me.'

The ropes parted. Mina slumped onto her paws with a groan of relief, gulping ragged breaths as delicious as cool spring water. She shivered as Torven tenderly licked her wounds clean, *rough-warm-damp* rasping over the raw gashes. 'Thank you.' She nuzzled against his flank. 'Are we friends?'

He grinned. 'We sure ain't enemies. I lost a brother to Man's wires last spring. You stole two of his chickens two moons ago. I watched you. Very cunning.'

She blushed, draping her brush over her eyes in embarrassment. The wolf laughed. 'There's a rabbit warren close to the rocks by Three Ponds. You're

24

welcome to hunt there; they're far too gristly for our cubs.'

They touched noses. 'I'll remember this kindness,' Mina smiled.

He bowed his head. 'Travel safe, miss. May the sun always shine upon you.' Then he turned and trotted into the trees.

The full moon kissed the frozen pines as Mina returned from the warren, her belly sated with a stupid buck who'd been caught dozing in the open. Her throat still burned from that terrible struggle hours before, but the meat was a pleasant ache that warmed her bones.

A faint whimper sliced through the silence. Her ears twitched: beyond the ridge. She padded over the frozen earth, as silently as her laboured breathing would allow. In the gloom, she made out a birch tree badly scratched on one side. Too high for badger claws, too low for deer antlers.

Her neckfur prickled. The icy feeling of every prey in a forest: the feeling of being watched.

Something lay at the foot of the boulder.

The cub-watcher. Its flank had been ripped open, its throat torn to pulp. In the chewed-up earth she found tracks: rounder than a wolf's, their outline blurred by fur.

Lynx.

Rising, Mina peered into the darkness. Nothing.

Odd for a lynx to attack a full-grown wolf. Mostly they hunted hares and squirrels, not fearsome brawny predators like this.

A whine from beyond the boulder. Fear prickled her guts like thorns.

The cubs.

Because of course. The lynx must have smelled the cubs, and the cub-watcher had leapt to their defence. It had put up a desperate fight to save the cubs.

And paid with its life.

Mina crept through the tunnel into a wide earthy hollow. A gleam of yellow eyes. A fluffy huddle shrank from her, trembling.

She whined to reassure the cubs, wagging her tail. But they were terrified. She was a stranger, and they'd just lost their uncle.

Backing out, she emerged from the den – to glimpse a large shadow bound away from the slaughtered wolf.

She skittered after it, bristling with fury. *Clear off!* Her snarl ended in a coughing fit that choked her throat like pond slime.

The lynx leapt into a tree and draped over a branch, lashing its tail.

Mina tried barking for help, but only managed a feeble croak. The night was warm, the sickly-sweet stink of the slaughtered cub-watcher thick in her throat. The carcass lay so close she could touch it.

Too close. She should drag it further off, so the lynx could feed in peace. Let it take the dead to sate its hunger, and leave the living.

But while she was doing that, it might come for the cubs. She raised her hackles.

A twig cracked behind her. She whirled around. Saw only the boulder. But lynx are superb climbers: they leap on their prey from above . . .

There! The lynx crouched in the shadows, cruel eyes glittering. Odd that her arrival hadn't frightened it off. Lynx rarely attack other hunters; they hunt by night, targeting the young and the sick.

The lynx dropped silently from the branch and began to prowl.

Mina raised her muzzle and shrieked a long warning that clawed at her injured throat: *Help!* Another spasm of coughing racked her body. Black spots danced before her eyes. Her throat burned. Her breath rasped like the crackle of dry leaves.

Then the horrid realisation dawned. The lynx knew she was injured. It had heard it in her voice and smelled it in her rank fur stench. Like the cubs, she was simply prey.

A movement at the corner of her eye. Two stubby muzzles emerging from the mouth of the den. She barked a warning: *Uff!* Danger!

The muzzles shrank back inside.

A distant howl quivering on the wind, echoed from many throats. *The pack!* Mina's heart leapt.

The lynx bared its teeth and hissed. Began circling. Fully twice her size, a mass of bristling muscle and tawny fur. Sharp fangs gleamed. And when the cubs nosed their way out again . . . the lynx would be on them.

Mina edged back into the mouth of the den. Planted her paws into the frosty earth, legs braced like a mighty oak. She would guard the cubs until the pack returned, or die trying. *One good bite*, she thought. *I should get one good crunch in before he tears me throat out.*

The lynx slunk closer. Tail lashing. Eyes glittering. Mina reared up, her jaws bared in a final defiant scream—

A blurred shadow exploded out of the frozen pines; before the lynx could even breathe Torven had bowled it over, two other juveniles snapping furiously at it. The lynx clawed and yowled but Torven lunged, and his jaws were deep in its throat, and he ripped upwards . . .

. . . and the lynx's life came away in his teeth.

A breathless silence fell. The other panting wolves were staring at Mina, hackles raised. She gazed back, swaying with exhaustion as the blood-fury leached from her bones. The lead female sniffed the meat that had been the cub-watcher.

A whine broke the hushed stillness. The cubs appeared at the mouth of the den. The lead wolf's hackles lowered, and she bounded past Mina to greet the cubs. Then another. And another. Mina's legs wobbled under her, and she slumped into the icy mud.

A cold wet nose nuzzled into her ear. Then thick grey fur curled around her back, sheltering her battered bones from the winter's chill. *Rough-warm-damp* brushed over her brow.

'Took yer bloody time about it,' she rasped in relief.

'Nice to see you too, Miss Scrounger,' Torven grinned.

4
FIGHT NIGHT

The vixen's scream tore the darkness, her screech echoing over the fields. Kane yelped and loped along on the floodtide of his lust. Above him the wind hissed through the beech trees, the warm reek of Oakley Farm swine too distant to mask the vixen's maddening scent. From the surrounding hedgerows came answering barks of other foxes hurrying to the gathering.

The church tower loomed black in the twilight. Before him the vixen's keening music raked his innards like claws. The shrill wails of rival suitors rose from the shadows all around.

He squeezed through the snarl of brambles out into the cemetery. His rivals snapped insults across the tombstones as the tawny vixen sprawled amid dead leaves. There she lay, a phantom of soft fire bathed in strong musky fragrance. The gleam of her golden eyes held the moonlight. Eight foxes had answered her call.

Wendell, a hulking veteran crisscrossed with silver scars, swaggered forwards. 'What do they call you?'

'Nightshade,' she purred.

He hopped onto a stone crypt, swelled with arrogance. 'Well, Nightshade, I'm Wendell the Warrior. My name is whispered with awe from Brook Bridge to the crossroads. Against me, grown foxes turn to frightened cubs. I'm smoke before the hounds. There's no one swifter nor braver.' He glared about him. The others shrank back, lowered their eyes or pretended to nip their bellies for ticks. They knew Wendell's fearsome reputation. 'Anybody foolish enough to challenge me?'

'Mylo will!' A young juvenile trotted forwards, green eyes slitted. 'I've grabbed conies by the warrenful, and snatched a dozen plump chickens from under the noses of dozy dogs. I may only be four winters old, but I'm quick 'n' fierce.' He bowed his head to Nightshade. 'I'll fight this bag o' bones for your beauty, milady!'

His rivals jeered their scorn. 'Cluck, cluck!' Vennic chuckled. 'The Terror of the Chicken Runs ain't fit to lick my scats!'

'I disagree,' Taymar smirked. 'This young whelp's welcome to my scat anytime. But if I were

Mylo I'd get my arse outta here. *Now*, while he still can.'

A surge of rage lifted Mylo's hackles. 'Oh yeah?' He glared at Wendell. 'We gonna fight, old-timer, or are ya just wind 'n' piss?'

Wendell turned away with a flick of his brush. 'Insolent cub!' he sneered. 'You've the heart of a rabbit and the strength of a mouse. The night's a big place – go hide in it, fleabrain!'

Mylo bared his teeth. 'Make me . . . *Scat-eater*.'

Wendell rounded on him, lips peeled back in a terrible scream. '*You'll pay for that!*' They lunged at each other, grappling and tearing as their snarls echoed across the cemetery. Mylo had youth and speed in his favour, darting under Wendell's jaws to snap at his throat. But Wendell outmatched him in both strength and experience; whenever his fangs struck, blood flowed. Soon Mylo was limping from a dozen ragged wounds, his forelegs gashed, his nose torn. Staggering away he slumped into the earth, wheezing.

The onlookers exchanged glances. Some of them sniggered uneasily. 'All right, Wendell,' Vennic called. 'Let him be. He's had enough.'

Wendell sat back on his haunches. 'Well, you stupid cub? Learnt your lesson?'

Mylo growled and lurched up on shaky legs.

'Why . . . you gettin' tired, badger-breath?'

Wendell snarled and lunged, pinning Mylo as he writhed in the dirt. 'You can't win, cub! Yield!'

Mylo twisted and sank his teeth into Wendell's forepaw. Wendell roared and scuttled back as Mylo wrenched free. 'Never!' He bared bloody fangs. 'Ain't done yet, slobberchops. C'mon then!'

Kane shook his head as the two foxes clashed once again. *Bow out*, he silently urged Mylo. *Stand down. There's no need to keep fighting.* Yet still Mylo rose, panting raggedly now as he swiped at Wendell with weary paws. Murmurs of admiration arose from the circle of onlookers. Twice he had fallen and twice risen again, bloody but unbowed.

With a powerful wrench of his shoulders Wendell slammed his challenger into the earth. '*Enough!* Know when you're beat.'

Mylo spat blood into his eyes. 'Eat scat, snaggletooth!'

With a bellow of rage Wendell pounced, his fangs crunching deep into Mylo's throat. Mylo yelped and flailed desperately, eyes bulging as his claws raked Wendell's torso. But still Wendell clung on, teeth latched into Mylo's windpipe as the younger fox rasped for air. Wendell shook his head this way and that, heaving Mylo's battered body off the ground and smashing him down, as if he were a feeble rabbit squealing its last.

'That's enough, Wendell!' Taymar urged. 'You've beaten him!'

Nightshade hopped onto the plinth. 'He fought bravely,' she murmured. 'Let him free.'

Mylo struggled feebly, sobbing for breath as Wendell tightened his grip. 'Had enough?' he growled through a mouthful of fur.

A hushed pause, then . . .

'. . . I yield,' Mylo gurgled. Wendell slowly opened his jaws; Mylo slumped into the earth, dazed and bleeding as he cowered at Wendell's feet. His whimpers echoed around the clearing.

'Get this snivelling whelp out of my sight,' hissed Wendell. Vennic helped Mylo hobble among the tombstones to lick his ragged injuries. Chest heaving, Wendell glared about him. 'Anyone else? No?' He snorted derisively, then turned to smile at Nightshade. 'Now, milady, it's high time we—'

'Oi!'

All eyes turned as Kane trotted into the clearing. 'Why don'tcha pick on someone your own size?'

Wendell sniggered. 'Come to clean up his sorry mess, hmm?'

Kane ignored him, gently nuzzling Mylo back onto his feet. 'C'mon, mate. Rest easy – I got ya.'

'Look at the pair of 'em!' Wendell sneered. 'A

snivelling cub and his nurse, hah!' Behind him Nightshade uncurled atop her stone throne, tight-lipped with revulsion.

'He's a braver fighter than you'll ever be!' Kane spat. 'You ain't worthy to lick his paws!'

Nightshade's eyes widened. 'A fresh challenge!' She settled down to watch. 'And what'll *you* do, young 'un?'

Kane bowed his head gallantly. 'Lady, you grace us with your presence. I've come to claim my prize.'

She laughed. 'Spare me the flattery.'

Kane smirked. 'Not to seem rude, but I actually meant' – his head turned – '*him.*'

Wendell bristled. 'Oh really?' He stalked forwards. 'Run back to yer hidey-hole, prattling wretch – before I rip yer tongue out!'

Kane stood his ground. 'Come get it, moss-muncher!'

Wendell began circling, hackles raised. 'You dare challenge me?! The blood of noble warriors runs through my veins!'

Kane snorted. 'Really? Who was it, then: your wormtailed father, or your frogfaced mother?'

Stung by the insult, Wendell bellowed with rage and charged. Kane smiled grimly. Flexing his limbs, he hurled himself like an uncoiled viper at

Wendell. Locked together, both creatures rolled over and over. Loam and leaves sprayed in all directions as they bit, grappled and kicked, raking each other with heavy claws. Blood speckled the gravestones. Tattered wisps of russet fur fluttered to earth.

They broke apart. Wendell arched his back, bared his teeth and gekkered with rage. Showing neither fear nor hesitation, Kane grinned at his enemy.

Wendell gave a blood-curling growl, leering at his opponent. 'You're bold to face me, insolent fleabag! Nobody's ever bested me. Your heart is mine!'

Kane smirked. 'Yours? Sorry, can't have it.' He winked at Nightshade, who blushed. 'It's promised to a fair pretty maid!'

Wendell glared. 'What's *wrong* with you?' He swung his muzzle toward Mylo's quivering body. 'You'd rather die for that whimpering cub, someone you don't even *know?!*'

Kane squared his shoulders. 'A jeering coward beating a fighter who's already down . . . while everyone else watches? And you wanna know what's wrong with *me?*' He hunkered protectively in front of Mylo's trembling form. 'Yeah, I'd rather die . . . so *bring it on!*'

He thundered in like a raging juggernaut. They

crashed together, twisting and snapping, their claws slashing at each other's faces. For the first time in his life, Wendell felt cold fear. He was larger and stronger, yet hopelessly outmatched by Kane's power and fury; now Wendell was bloodied and weary while Kane was fresh and angry; now, he was fighting for his life. The seasoned veteran tried to twist free from the enraged youngster, but to no avail. His breath sobbed raggedly in his throat as he strained and writhed in vain. Agony tore through him as Kane's teeth sank deep into his hindleg.

Suddenly Wendell whirled around and swept a pawful of soil into Kane's eyes!

Temporarily blinded, Kane yelped and lurched away. Seizing his chance, Wendell squirmed free, gulping blessed lungfuls of air. With a savage howl of triumph he charged at his floored enemy, eyes blazing, jaws agape.

Through a muddy haze, Kane saw him coming. He fell backwards, a wild yell ripping from his throat. Then Wendell's full weight fell upon him as Kane thrust upward mightily with his paws in a stupendous burst of power.

All four paws slammed squarely into Wendell's body. The fox shot high in the air, screaming as he crashed down onto the tomb's hard granite edge.

The onlookers watched wide-eyed as Kane

staggered upright, breathing heavily. He glared at the huddled figure on the ground. Wendell uncurled, groaning as agony seared up his spine.

Kane trotted forwards, eyes narrowed. 'Hurts, doesn't it? Being in pain. Being *afraid*.'

Wendell's eyes darted around in dismay. 'No . . . you foxes, stop him! Nnngh . . . I'm still in charge here . . . do as I say!'

Silence. Then Vennic spat upon the ground. 'No.'

Wendell gazed about in disbelief, into a wall of stony faces. All around him was a circle of contemptuous onlookers. High above, a velvet sky dusted with a thousand mocking stars. His authority had been chipped away piece by piece; now he lay battered and helpless.

'We ain't scared of you no more!' Taymar snarled.

Wendell stared back, horrified. 'Nobody was stronger than me . . . I was the leader . . . I was mighty . . .' He gazed beseechingly up at Nightshade. 'Milady . . . please . . .'

Nightshade turned away, her face pinched in disgust.

Kane prowled forwards. 'Aye, and look where that got ya. Who saw you beat a defenceless cub down? Everyone. And who wants to help you now?'

Silence in the cemetery.

'Yeah, none of 'em,' Kane grinned. 'Nobody likes you. They wouldn't piss on you if you were on fire! You're all alone now.' He crouched low, teeth bared. 'Run away, you stinking coward. Run away . . . and *never* return!'

With the jeering taunts of his rivals echoing in his ears, Wendell limped away into the darkness. Broken. Bloody. Defeated. Taymar and Vennic padded over to Mylo and began gently licking his wounds clean.

'Look after him,' Kane said, and trotted towards the church. Nightshade drew alongside him.

'Want some company?'

'I thought you'd never ask,' Kane smiled, and Nightshade leaned against him as they went into the moonlight.

5
CUB CAPERS

'Marlo! Eska! What've I told you about fighting?!'

Shandar loomed over her squabbling children. Both fox cubs froze in a jumble of tawny fur, Marlo chewing on Eska's ear while his sister gnawed his forepaw. 'We were just practicing biting and clawing,' Eska beamed, then yelped as Marlo nipped her again.

Shandar hauled her son off by his neck-scruff. 'Marlo, you wanna grow up into a big strong dog fox, don't you? Young foxes don't get into silly scraps and they *certainly* don't fight their sisters!'

Marlo scowled at his sister. 'I didn't do anyfink. *She* started it!'

Eska glared down her nose with icy scorn. 'Ladies do *not* start fights – but they can *finish* them!'

'*Children*,' Shandar growled. Both cubs shrank against her, mewing in apology. Her gaze softened as they nuzzled her flank. 'Look,' she sighed, 'why don't you just . . . go and play. *Try* not to claw each other's eyes out before I get back. Okay?'

'Yes, Mum,' Eska preened, taking extra care to tread on Marlo's brush as she minced away.

Marlo glared after her. Shandar nudged him along with her snout. 'Run along now. Be nice to your sister. I'll bring supper later.'

'Yes, Mum,' he grinned, and scampered after Eska.

'Try this,' Marlo urged her closer. Eska narrowed her eyes over the steaming cowpat sprinkled with shiny black specks.

'You're a fibber! That's yucky!'

'I ain't.' Marlo snapped up a beetle, his teeth cracking the hard shell. 'Chomp-chomp! Now you try 'em!' Eska's eyes gleamed. She dug in greedily.

'Euugh!'

Eska recoiled and spat out a mouthful of dung. Marlo streaked away, giggling. 'Beetles good, dung bad. Heehee!'

Eska raced after him. 'No fair! Stinky Face!'

They tumbled and wrestled down the muddy lane, swatting at each other with their paws and nipping each other's tails. Thrushes spilled from the blackthorns and skimmed away over the fields, and

41

droning bees burrowed into the foxgloves as both cubs passed by. Suddenly the bitter stink of woodsmoke washed over them, soured with the pungent stench of sweat. Marlo's nose wrinkled.

'Man,' he bristled, voice trembling with excitement. 'All those juicy leftovers! Tasty scraps!'

Eska shrank back. 'No no! Mum said we're not allowed! Humans bad, they're scary!' Her mother's hushed tales prickled her guts with icy dread, for humans ripped open the earth to feed their ravenous hunger. They tore down mighty trees to choke the meadows under black rivers of oily tar. Humans spread death and fear wherever they roamed: with their long grey sticks that spat white flames of death; their monstrous snarling beasts that belched foul smoke on the black stinking rivers; their mobs of howling hounds that flooded the open moors under the bugle's haunting wail.

Marlo grinned. 'Big plump chickens! Fat juicy sausages! Crunchy bacon!' His ears twitched eagerly. 'C'mon, it'll be fun!'

Eska huddled against the hedge, trembling. 'No! It's not safe!'

Marlo's smile faded, and he trotted back to curl up beside her. 'I'll stay right with you,' he murmured. 'We'll go together. In 'n' out, real quick.

Me 'n' you. Okay?'

Eska nuzzled against him. 'Promise?'

Marlo licked her cheek. 'Promise!'

A breathless pause . . . then Eska nodded. 'Okay.'

Brother and sister crept side by side to the vast looming farmhouse. A catflap yawned before them. Marlo poked his head inside, then grinned back at her. 'Looks clear, c'mon!'

They slunk into a hallway of cold stone, the rich scent of roasting meat washing over them. Metal scraped behind a closed door to their right. Eska winced as her stomach growled, but Marlo was already creeping left to peer around the corner. He ducked back, eyes wide.

'Cat!'

Eska shivered against him. Horrid yowling monsters of slashing claws and sharp fangs that preyed on bumbling mice. Hardly daring to breathe, she peeked around the corner. Two sagging armchairs before the crackling log fire. A small plate speckled with crumbs.

And a grey-striped cat dozing on the rug.

Quiet as mice, they crept to the nearest armchair, hardly daring to breathe . . .

A floorboard creaked!

The cat's ear flickered. Marlo shrank behind the armchair, Eska huddled against him.

They waited. Nothing. The cat dozed on.

'Through here,' Marlo whispered, leading his sister into the corridor.

Heavy footsteps approaching. They froze. Trapped out in the open. Marlo's eyes darted around, then fixed onto the half-open door leading into yawning blackness.

'C'mon!' he whispered. 'Downstairs!' Eska hurried after him, scurrying down the cold stone steps into the gloom.

They stopped.

And stared.

They stood and gaped, noses twitching, their eyes shining like stars, so overwhelmed they couldn't speak. A glorious paradise for hungry animals.

A vast underground cellar stretched before them. Shelves reaching from floor to ceiling on three sides, the end wall filled with dozens of huge flagons of golden cider. Both side walls piled high with rows of the finest fattest geese, plump juicy chickens and succulent young ducks, plucked and ready for roasting! And high above, dangling from the rafters were at least twenty magnificent smoked hams and a dozen sides of bacon!

Marlo whirled joyfully. 'We've done it!' he yipped. 'We'll never be hungry again. Mum'll be so proud of us!' Eska danced around him, giggling with glee. They raced over to the lowest shelf, tugged down a plump chicken between them and eagerly tore into the delicious pink meat.

'Don't bolt your food, slobberchops!' Marlo teased through a mouthful of chicken.

Eska spat a bone at him. 'Shuddup, Stinky Face!' she laughed.

The cellar door creaked open! They froze, horrorstruck as blinding golden light poured over them like a cloudburst.

'Hide, sis!' Marlo hissed. He and Eska scrambled into the darkness, jumped onto a low shelf and crouched behind the row of huge glass bottles. Peering through the gaps, they saw a thickset woman in a dirty apron stomping down the stairs.

With a giant rolling pin in one hand.

At the foot of the stairs she paused. Sighed heavily at the mess of shredded meat and gnawed bones littering the floor. 'That darn cat again.' She glanced left. Glanced right. Then she shrugged and headed straight for their shelf!

The cubs shrank together, trembling with dread. Only a thin row of bottles concealed them. The woman halted directly in front of their hiding place. Her heavy breathing rasped through the musky air. Marlo tensed as the housekeeper took a flagon off their shelf and tucked it under a flabby arm. Just two spaces away.

'How many drinks tonight, ma'am?' she called upstairs.

'I dunno, Susan,' a sharp voice answered. 'A couple, I guess.'

'Yes, ma'am.' The housekeeper pulled a second flagon from the shelf, right next to the cubs' hiding place.

If she takes one more, she'll see us! Marlo thought. Eska huddled against him, quivering with fright.

The housekeeper paused.

'He drank three yesterday, ma'am.'

'All right. Take three, then.'

No! Icy dread flooded through Marlo's veins.

The housekeeper grabbed the cubs' flagon. Eska closed her eyes. Marlo bared his teeth, ready to spring . . .

'No, wait.'

The housekeeper paused, her hand wrapped around their bottle.

'Three's too many,' the voice sighed. 'It's unhealthy. Bill gets cranky when he's drunk. Just bring two.'

The housekeeper frowned. 'But maybe another, just in case—'

'Two's *plenty*, Susan. He'll only be out for a couple hours. Says them foxes are bound to come skulkin' for food anyway. Then he'll catch 'em and string 'em up on the front porch!'

'Dirty blighters,' the housekeeper muttered to herself. 'Get what's comin' to 'em.'

'You'll get their tails for your bedroom wall, Susan. Hurry up with them ciders now!'

'Yes, ma'am,' Susan trudged across the cellar and waddled back up the steps, a bottle under each arm.

And left the door open.

'Quick!' Marlo whispered. 'Before she comes back!' He leapt off the shelf and darted up the cellar stairs, Eska close behind. They squeezed through the narrow gap and crept through the corridor. The scrape of plates from the kitchen. Running water. Marlo slunk back into the living room, over the empty rug before the crackling fireplace.

The empty rug.

No cat.

Suddenly he was slammed sideways, choking for breath as he was pinned helplessly on the floor. Cruel claws sank deep into his fur. Eska shrank against the wall, horrified.

'Run, sis!' Marlo barked. 'Save yourself!' He twisted and writhed but struck nothing. The cat

47

hunkered over him, whiskers brushing his ear. Her gleaming green eyes narrowed to slits.

'Can *you* run?' she purred, voice dripping with malice. '*I think not!*'

Eska was rooted to the spot. Her brother trapped on the floor as the cat loomed over him. The cat flap yawning before her. The open yard to freedom. Safety.

'*Run!*' Marlo gasped, then yelped as the cat's claws sank deeper.

'Yesss!' she screeched, eyes glittering in triumph. 'Run, little princess! Run back to your hidey-hole, like the coward you are!'

Eska bared her teeth. Searing rage boiled through her.

Get off my brother!

She charged.

Before the cat could even snarl Eska crashed into her, jaws crunching deep into her hindleg. She fell sprawling, hissing and spitting as Marlo wriggled free. The cat rounded on them, fangs bared as she hissed with rage. Playtime was over. But now she was faced with two snarling enemies who snapped and clawed at her. She pounced, claws flashing. But Eska darted aside, raking her soft underbelly. Then she yowled as Marlo's teeth crunched deep into her tail. This was impossible! No prey had ever dared challenge her.

The tap shut off. 'What the hell's goin' on?' the housekeeper called out. 'You okay, Bella?'

The growling cubs advanced on her, hackles raised. Bloodied but unbowed.

Bella's nerve failed her. She retreated, ears flattened as she mewed for mercy.

Marlo puffed out his chest and barked. Turning tail, Bella streaked up the stairs to safety.

A hulking shadow appeared in the doorway, brandishing a broom.

'Filthy varmints!' Susan shrieked. 'Outta my house, ya stinkin' vermin!'

'Quick!' Marlo yelled. 'Outside now!' They dashed between Susan's legs, dodging the wild slashes of her broom. Together they raced into the hallway and burst through the cat flap to freedom!

A maddened scramble across the yard, through the hedge into the meadow. They collapsed into the shade of a towering oak, giggling helplessly with excitement.

'Let's *never* do that again,' Eska panted. Marlo nodded feebly, then growled with relief as Eska curled around him, licking his ragged wounds.

'Mum's gonna be so mad with us,' she groaned, slumping onto the damp leaves. Marlo nodded mournfully.

Then he grinned. 'Awful nice chicken though, weren't it?'

Eska's eyes glazed over in bliss. 'Yummy!' Marlo squirmed closer, nuzzling against her.

'Sorry I teased you,' he mumbled. 'Thanks for saving me, sis.'

Eska nibbled his ear affectionately. 'You're still a Stinky Face. But you're *my* Stinky Face.'

6
URBAN OUTLAWS

London in the rain. Ugh. Typical.

Grey sheets of water tumbled from the churning black sky, breaking upon the pavements with a thunderous roar. Howling wind buffeted the rain this way and that, spattering it under porches, cornices and capstones, drowning every possible refuge in freezing spray. Water was everywhere, crashing off the tarmac, swirling along gutters, pouring down drains. It flooded the city's cisterns, cascading through pipes, thundering across rooftops, staining the brickwork like sweeping washes of blood. It drowned the streets in a chill white mist. It dripped through ceiling cracks to trickle down walls, seeping into the bones of their cowering inhabitants.

Birds shivered in flimsy nests beneath gables and eaves, rocked by harsh jolts of icy sleet. In dark lairs underground, rats huddled listening to the endless drumming overhead. In rainswept suburbs, men and women bolted fast the shutters and clustered around their guttering fires with steaming mugs of tea. In lonely office blocks, late-night workers snapped window blinds shut, turned radiators up high and fled to their desks, hunched over keyboards as the rain thundered all about them.

Birds, rats, people: all safely undercover. Who could blame them? The streets were deserted, all of London shut indoors. It was almost midnight and the storm raged on.

No one in their right mind would be out on such a miserable night as this. You'd have to be a complete *idiot*.

Ho hum.

Somewhere amid the biting rain was a crossroads, a granite plinth crowned with a mounted statue. The man waved a sword, his face frozen in a heroic cry. The horse reared up, perhaps signalling dramatic defiance, perhaps preparing to hurl itself into battle. Perhaps just trying to dislodge the fat bloke off its back. We'll never know. But see: sheltered under the horse's belly, hunkered down against the spitting torrent – a lone grizzled fox.

Grey eyes gazed out into the sheeting downpour.

The old fox pretended not to notice the bitter wind that rippled his sodden fur. Only the downward tilt of his ears signalled any discomfort. One ear twitched; otherwise the creature might have been carved from stone.

The wind moaned. The endless rain hammered down. The fox tucked his brush in grimly and watched the murky street. An ambulance splashed past, its bright blue lights flashing.

Time trickled on.

He waited.

Gradually the rain lessened, and slowed, and stopped. The clouds parted; feeble moonlight dribbled down. The wet cobbles glittered under the orange streetlights, and every puddle held its own captive star.

A flicker of movement in the drenched emptiness; something crept out from the shadow of a parked car. It paused, a dark smudge in the hazy gloom, then darted out from the pavement and streaked across the road, headed straight for the statue.

The fox didn't move an inch.

The black streak reached the plinth and slowed to a trot, revealing an elegant tawny vixen with gleaming golden eyes. She halted before the fox, shook herself vigorously.

A shower of water spattered into his face.

'Thanks for that, Roxelle,' he sniffed. 'You must've noticed I wasn't quite soaked enough.'

'Couldn't help myself, Arren.' The vixen nonchalantly scratched her ear with a hindleg. 'Gotta keep myself entertained somehow.' She hopped up alongside him and yawned.

Arren gnawed her ear. 'So where've you been, anyway? You're two hours late.'

Roxelle nodded mournfully. 'False alarm back at the den. Pair o' cubs thought they'd seen something. Had to search the *whole* place out thoroughly before giving the all-clear. Silly mutts – of course I had to discipline them.'

'Nipped their tails, huh?'

A smirk flickered across Roxelle's muzzle. 'Something like that.'

He shifted over to make room. She snuggled closer with a weary huff.

'Can't really blame 'em.' Arren licked her cheek. 'They're jumpy. It's all this rain. Wears your bones down soon enough.'

Roxelle glanced sideways. 'Your bones too, Arren?'

He shrugged. '*I'm* all right.' He arched his back in a big luxuriant stretch, the warming thrill that washes from whisker-tip to tail-tuft. 'Aaahhh, that's better. Nope, I've seen way worse than this, and so've you.'

She whined and shivered against him. 'My pads are freezing. Can't stand all this cold!'

'Winter's sharp teeth,' he grinned. 'Curl up against this bag o' bones, young mouse!' Roxelle snorted and nuzzled her snout under his chin. The comforting beat of her heart against his ribs.

'It's so *boring* after sunset,' she growled. 'Nothing to do but root through trash and hunt rats. When're we gonna see some real action?'

Arren rolled his eyes. 'Soon enough, missie. Plenty of rich pickings by the docks. Ready for some lessons from a worn-out old dog?' His stomach gurgled.

Roxelle giggled. 'Best be off, then! Don't want to miss dinner, O wise toothless sage?'

Arren wriggled upright. 'Certainly not, cheeky pup!'

The vixen danced around him, teasing. 'Want me to stun an earthworm for you? Maybe a sleeping frog – yowch!'

Arren nipped her tail. 'This old dog's got some teeth yet. Now keep up, young scamp, or you'll eat my scats!'

Roxelle whisked away up the street. 'Race you there, old timer!'

Slumped behind his desk, the night guard jabbed idly at his phone. Fang the wolfhound dozed at his feet, paws twitching as he chased squealing rabbits through his dreams. The guard slouched back in his chair, glaring sullenly at the muted TV headlines. Trouble for High Street retail, some celeb bullshit, politicians looking shifty. Nothing new there. Only 12:05 . . . jeez. Another mindless half-hour watching the world slide by outside, then lockup and a brisk walk round the block before home to bed. Damn dog needs his exercise anyway.

'Why not around the front?'

'Too open. Too noisy. Besides, litter bins aren't easy to raid. Better to hit the back-alley rubbish skips instead.'

'It can't be *that* simple!'

'Sure is,' Arren smirked. They padded into the alleyway's yawning mouth, slimy brick walls towering either side. Insects circled beneath a flickering lamp; Arren leapt up to crunch a moth in a single bound. 'Pretty good for an old bonebag, eh?'

Roxelle giggled. 'Bet that knocked ten sunsets off your life. Four winters already, haven't you?'

Arren grinned back. 'Five. If it's my time soon,

I'm ready. Everything has its time, and everything dies. Then I'll drift up to the Star Place and chase rabbits through the golden fields.'

'Wishful words, cub lullabies and silly omens,' Roxelle scoffed. 'Don't dwell on dream-tales, old warrior.' She shuddered as a terrier yapped two streets away. 'Blasted hounds! Whenever they come, we run, badgers run, rabbits run – everyone runs.'

'But not here,' Arren soothed. 'City dogs are kennelled, or leashed, or chained up tight. They won't be roaming the streets, hunting us scavengers. We're safe, eh?'

Roxelle buried her muzzle into his flank. 'I suppose so.'

They crept through the shadows as silent as moon wraiths, noses quivering at the glorious street smells wafting all around them. Warm yeasty air belched from doors of bars and nightclubs, spiced with the sour reek of vomit and the sweet stink of garbage. A teenager sitting on the curb gawped at their silent shadows, giggled and keeled over, her beer bottle tinkling across the cobbles. Another figure tottered onto the pavement, groped for a lamppost, missed and sank to his knees with a drunken whoop.

Roxelle sniggered. 'Graceful as legless pigs,

ain't they?'

Arren chuckled. 'Surefooted as ducks on ice, bless 'em. C'mon!'

They splashed through puddles and squeezed through the hole in the chainlink fence. An overflowing rubbish skip gaped before them, bulging plastic bags torn at the seams as fallen scraps littered the ground. Arren craned up on his hindlegs to dig in eagerly. 'Mmmmff . . . chicken leg! Y'want some?'

Roxelle giggled through a mouthful of pizza crust. 'Thank the fates for humans, heehee!'

Fang tugged against his leash, nose twitching at the tempting scent of kebabs and burgers. The night guard jerked him back. 'Heel, boy!' Just one more circuit past the waterfront, then home to bed.

Suddenly Fang froze, ears twitching as he sniffed the air. Was it . . . Yes! A faint long-buried scent washed over him, ancient instincts prickling his nose. A dozen generations of long-dead grandsires who hunted howling wolves under frozen peaks, ran down snuffling badgers and ripped the life from squealing ferrets. But this . . .

Fox!

He strained forwards, barking eagerly. The guard sniggered. 'Got a scent, boyo? Get 'im, then. Go on!'

And unclipped the leash.

Fang tore into the darkness, baying with bloodlust. The hunt was on!

Both foxes trotted down to the foreshore, their paws crunching through the shingle. Out over the brown sludge tide, seagulls wailed beneath the moon.

Sated, Roxelle nuzzled into Arren's side with a contented huff. 'Still got the knack, old bonebag!'

Arren licked her cheek. 'Glad to hear it, famine chops—'

Fang's howl sliced through the night. Arren's head whipped around as Roxelle huddled against him. The distant skittering of claws on pebbles. 'Hound!' he hissed. 'Follow me, quick!' They streaked up the beach beneath the crumbling pier, onto a wide sunken jetty over the churning river. Salt-rotted planks hid the pale moon as Arren hopped onto a brine-soaked beam. They crept onward, ears pricked at every creak. Suddenly Arren jerked his paw back with a yelp of pain. 'Damn nails!' Dark spots speckling the rotten planks. He frantically licked his paw clean, desperate to staunch the bleeding . . .

A low rumbling growl. On their right. They sank onto their bellies, hardly daring to breathe. A hulking shadow lengthened against the moonlit wall . . .

The wolfhound prowled around the corner, sniffing the air for the delicious scent of blood. A mass of shaggy grey fur, slavering jaws and sunken black eyes. Both foxes shrank back into the shadows; Arren felt Roxelle quivering against him like a terrified cub. A fierce wave of affection pulsed through him. *If it finds us, I'll rip its throat out before it hurts her.*

'C'mon!' he whispered. They crawled together, quiet as mice.

A floorboard groaned!

Fang howled in triumph, icy panic flooding Arren's veins.

'RUN!' he barked, exploding from the shadows as Fang charged with bared teeth. They grappled together, Arren darting under the wolfhound's jaws to snap at his throat. Fang yelped and brushed him off with flailing claws. Arren sprang again, bowling him over into the muck.

'Arren!' Roxelle was frozen by the doorway, eyes wide with dread.

Arren whirled around. 'Go, Roxelle! GO NOW!'

Fang untwisted and sank his teeth deep into Arren's hindleg. Arren screamed. Fell. A flailing forepaw clubbed Fang's muzzle; he darted back out of reach, hackles bristling.

Arren uncurled with a groan. Fang began to circle, lips peeled back in a snarl. The wolfhound knew he was wounded and taunted him. Waiting to strike.

Everything has its time, and everything dies . . .

Arren struggled up onto shaky legs. Bared his teeth.

But not here. Not tonight!

Fang hunkered low, a deep bubbling growl between slavering jaws. Arren squared his shoulders and grunted like an old boar badger facing his end. *C'mon then, you stupid ugly mutt. I'm right here – come on!*

With a savage howl the monster leapt—

A tawny blur slammed into the wolfhound with a feral screech.

Roxelle! They locked together in the mud, snarling and tearing. Grit sprayed out as they bit, grappled and snapped, raking each other with heavy claws. Blood spattered into the mud. Roxelle scrambled upright as Fang flung himself upon her. She screamed as his jaws crunched into her flank—

Arren lunged forwards with a primal roar. He smashed into the wolfhound; Fang yelped as Arren savaged him with raging fury, driving him back across the rotted floorboards.

And straight over the edge.

Fang wailed as he fell. Down. Down. Down into the churning black depths.

Arren hobbled over to peer into the murky torrent. Nothing but the flicker of whitecaps as the river heaved beneath them. Roxelle nuzzled beneath his chin, tenderly licking his ragged wounds clean.

Arren managed a wheezing laugh. 'Reckon that's enough action for you tonight, missie?'

Roxelle nibbled his ear. 'Aw shuddup, you old bonebag!'

7
EYES ON THE PRIZE

Deep in his den Renard's stomach growled, jerking him awake. The golden light of sunset drifted down the tunnel; he'd been snoozing all day.

Quit lazing about, you idiot. Time to eat!

Padding up the tunnel, he emerged among a tangle of oak roots to sniff the warm sweet air. A myriad of delicious smells washed over him – sizzling meat, fresh bread, the sharp vinegar tang of fried fish. So many choices! So much opportunity!

Renard padded through the park, paws crunching the crinkled leaves. Suddenly a dark snuffling shape scuttled across his path. Earthspike the hedgehog bristled with anger and curled into a ball.

Renard trotted around him, smirking as he prodded the spines with a forepaw. 'C'mon, mate! I'm just passing through!'

'Go away!' a muffled voice grumbled. 'Dumb fox, leave me alone!'

'Aw, you ain't gonna be nice? Okay then.' Looming over the ball of prickles Renard cocked his leg.

And doused the hedgehog.

Sneezing and spluttering Earthspike uncurled. Too late. With a terrified squeal the life was crunched out of him. Renard lay amid the carpet of leaves, chewing slowly and spitting out the spines.

Not enough, his stomach gurgled. Just a measly morsel. East, then. He crept under the broken fence and through the row of parked cars, wrinkling his nose at the foul stink of grease and oiled rubber. Humans choked the earth with their filth, roared about in their metal monsters and vomited poison into the waterways.

At least they littered plenty, Renard thought. Hadn't eaten so well since he was a cub! He trotted through the lengthening shadows as the sun kissed the rooftops. On a wall opposite the pub sat a lean grey cat, licking its claws as if savouring the memory of its last prey. *Always be polite to cats*, his mother had told him. *The humans worshipped them as gods long ago; they've never forgotten this.*

'Lovely evening,' Renard smiled.

The cat paused its grooming. 'My, aren't *you* a handsome fellow,' she mewed. 'Your mother was clearly a vixen of good breeding.'

Renard blushed beneath his thick red fur. 'Thank you!'

The cat sank onto her belly. 'How d'you tear your ear?'

Renard shrugged. 'Oh, it's always been like this. My mother said it made me special.'

'Very dashing,' the cat purred. 'What are you called?'

'Renard.' He liked the way it flowed off his tongue like water.

The cat peered down at him with gleaming eyes. 'French, eh? You really *are* an uncommon fox, you know.' She licked a paw daintily. 'I'm Amelia.'

Renard cocked his head to one side. 'Amelia? How elegant. Most of the cats I've met have silly names like Tigger or Spots.'

'Amelia is a *proper* name for a lady,' the cat purred.

Renard grinned. 'Sounds like you're quite the popular dame around here, huh?'

Amelia scowled. 'Certainly not! Those filthy ginger tomcats loitering in the street every night, screeching their heads off and scrapping over rotten fish-heads! No elegance. No *class!*' She flicked her tail scornfully. 'Give me a proper gentleman who bathes twice a week, I say!'

Renard sensed that the conversation was

finished. 'Well, lovely to meet you, Amelia. I'm off to find some grub.'

'Try the market,' Amelia offered. 'Go along the towpath, under the bridge then across the road.' She stretched with a yawn. 'There's been a food festival today, you'll find quite the feast there.'

Renard's eyes widened. 'You aren't coming?'

Amelia preened herself. 'No thanks. I had some cod fillets before I came outside.'

Renard had no idea what cod was, so he just smiled politely.

'It's a fish with delicate white flesh,' Amelia purred. '*Quite* delicious.'

Renard was impressed. 'I've never eaten fish before.' His stomach gurgled in agreement.

'Well, happy hunting, Renard,' Amelia uncurled and vanished over the wall.

'Nice meeting you, Amelia!' Renard called, and trotted away through the shadows.

A blackbird scolded him from high above as he padded along the towpath, nose twitching at the delicious aroma of sizzling meat up ahead. The shadows crawled across the path as he paused to drink, the sunlit water ablaze with shimmering gold.

Footsteps! He shrank behind a bush as two figures jogged into view, their breath fogging the air. Renard watched as they puffed up the slope out of sight before he slunk warily under the bridge. Beer cans littered the underpass, a rumpled mess of fabric nestled in the shadows. Renard crept closer, sniffing the air . . .

An arm swung outward with a bleary groan. Renard yelped and darted back, scuttling out onto the towpath. He looked back; the rustling heap was turning over, settling down into slumber again.

He'd heard of them, the roaming humans unable to sleep with a roof over their heads. Imagine sleeping out under the open stars, in the cold wet dark! No safe warm burrow to call home! He shivered and hurried on.

Stop that, he chided himself. *It's just the evening chill. You're all on your own out in the city. Don't get attached. Trust only yourself. Caring's dangerous. It'll get you hurt.*

Dusk was falling; climbing the slope Renard slunk under a van, waited until a car rumbled by, then streaked across the road into the safety of a bus shelter. Twinkling lights had been draped across the street like cobwebs, and each puddle held its own captive jewel.

Scattered groups of people wandered through the open market, Renard trailing after them like a wisp of smoke. A package fell to the ground with a wet scrunch, spilling its warm contents onto the cobbles. 'Yew bloody idiot,' someone swore. 'We only just bought that. Pick it up!'

'I ain't touching nuffink! Unhygienic, thash what it is!'

Someone else swooped down to rescue a chip. 'Five-second rule, Bill! It's still good!'

'Fuck off.'

Renard waited until they had moved away, then darted out and tore open the damp paper. Mmm . . . fish and chips! Amelia would certainly be impressed.

''Ey, Bill. Look who's come out to play!'

'Cor, what a gent. 'E's eatin' your dinner, look!'

Bill slumped onto a bench, raising his bottle in a drunken salute. 'Yeah? Well it's yours now, mate. Enjoy it!' Laughing among themselves the group reeled off, singing raucously out of tune. Renard winced; tinkling birdsong it wasn't. He dragged his sodden prize back into the shadows and dug in eagerly.

The market slowly emptied, stragglers trickling away into the surrounding streets. Nobody noticed the lone fox gobbling the discarded takeaway outside a shuttered bookshop.

Renard snapped up the last mouthful of batter, stretching out with a blissful yawn. That was *delicious*! Far better than the mouldy scraps he often found in rubbish skips and bin-bags. His ears pricked as a large delivery van jolted past, the wonderful scent of roast meat tickling his nose. He chased after it, splashing through puddles and weaving around bollards as they crossed the town square.

A tangle of scaffolding towered above; Renard sprang upward, scrambling across duckboards and rusty pipes out onto the rooftops. Below him the van veered left, brake lights flaring. He quickened his pace, bounding across to a neighbouring gutter.

In that part of town the ancient houses huddled close together, their teetering gables almost touching above the street. Easy enough. Anyone peering out of their windows might have glimpsed a flash of russet lightning leaping from chimney pot to weathervane, streaking across the slates and gutters yet never putting a paw wrong. Renard raced over the dripping rooftops, keeping the van in sight. It burbled to a halt before the traffic lights, and he relaxed. No need to rush . . .

A plaintive mewing drifted through his ears. He slowed. Glanced down.

In a filthy yard below, a glossy black cat yowled pitifully as it scratched at the back door. Renard's stomach clenched, his mother's whispers echoing through his ears. *Don't intervene. It's not your concern. Caring will hurt you. Don't get involved.*

The delivery van idled before the red light. A ten-second conversation couldn't hurt, surely . . .

'Hey there! What's wrong?' Renard called down.

The cat turned a tearstained face up at him. 'My owner locked me out! His kid smacked me and pulled my tail – I only wanted to warn her!' He stalked back and forth. 'Just a little prick with my claws, and I'm shut out in the cold!'

Beneath the red light the van loitered. Unease squirmed in Renard's stomach; he should focus on the prize at hand, leave this sorry fool behind to wallow in his own misery. It'd only slow him down.

The cat craned up on his hindlegs, staring beseechingly up at the single lamp through the second-floor window. 'Please!' he pleaded. 'It was an accident! She hurt me – what else could I do? Please let me in.'

The lamp went out. Darkness fell. The cat curled up with a groan.

Don't get involved. It's not your concern.

The traffic light turned orange. The van's engine growled into life.

DON'T GET INVOLVED –

Dammit.

70

Renard hopped onto the shed roof, then down onto a stack of damp pallets. Distantly he heard the van rumble away down the street, and ignored it. The cat turned his sorrowful gaze on him, then buried his face into his flank.

'You all right?' Renard asked.

The cat sighed into his pillow of dark fur. 'Take a wild guess,' he mumbled.

Renard trotted close to curl around him. 'Hey, now. It's okay. Come daybreak they'll forget about it. This'll all blow over.' He glanced around. 'Now where's your bed?'

'Inside,' the cat muttered. 'Everything's inside . . . except me. My soft bed, my chew-toys.' He sighed. 'What I wouldn't give fer a nice bowl o' fish right now . . .'

A grey tail vanishing over a wall . . .

'I had some cod fillets before I came outside . . .'

Renard grinned. 'You like fish, huh?'

A dreamy look washed over the cat's face. 'I *love* it. Best thing in the world!'

Renard hopped onto the shed roof. 'Lucky you. There's someone in my neighbourhood who's right up your street, lad!'

The cat sprang up beside him. 'Come off it! What'd she ever want with a fuzzy old tom like me?'

71

'Depends – how often d'you wash?'

The cat blinked sheepishly. 'Every day. Why?'

Renard grinned. 'Oh, she's gonna *love* you!'

8
THROUGH STAR-KISSED STREETS

The storm had passed barely an hour ago, sweeping east downriver and fading out over the Thames estuary. London sparkled gold, silver and electric blue neon, and puddles jewelled Chelsea's deserted streets. In the Royal Hospital gardens moonlight glittered on the wet shrubs, and a nightingale ruffled its feathers and serenaded the park from an oak branch.

Joris ignored it. The young fox was hunkered down beneath a parked car with his ears pricked, for a vixen had screeched among the trees and set his hackles quivering. Lust corkscrewed through his belly and sank its claws deep. He shrank back and whimpered as an ambulance splashed past and swerved out of sight. Then the shrill scream rose from the shadows again and he barked in reply.

Bushes rustled as she emerged, ghosting from the

park into the street and sniffing the air. Joris's heart sang as he gazed upon her. Her coat was the lustrous reddish-brown of autumn beech leaves, her eyes two green leaves that flashed in the night. The rain had lent her fur a pale sheen of silver, and her musky aroma soaked his senses. She was beautiful.

He uncurled and trotted out from his refuge. The vixen gazed evenly back. 'And who are you, young gent?'

Joris swaggered before the vixen. 'I'm your best suitor, milady.' He twitched his brush. 'You have a beautiful voice.'

Green eyes twinkled. 'You're that tod who hangs around the bakery over the river, aren't you?'

Joris preened his chest. 'I am. You're a smart girl, sweetheart. What gave me away?'

'Those black tufts on your ears,' she grinned, flashing teeth as white as hazelnut kernels. 'That white star on your chest. *And*,' she wrinkled her nose, 'the stink from their rubbish bins. Real memorable.' She padded into the shelter of the pavement wall and curled up.

Joris blinked, his confidence wavering as he nosed after her. *Don't let her knock your game. Turn up the charm!* 'I'll give you anything you desire.' He leapt up onto the garden wall and flashed his most alluring smile, the kind that always made the vixens giggle and flutter their eyelashes. 'You name it, I'll provide it.'

The vixen smiled and shook her head. 'No need – I mean, thanks and all that – but it's fine. I'm good.'

Suddenly a door opened; golden lamplight flooded the porch, a cat yowled and a voice answered, but the wall-top was now deserted.

Down the street both foxes courted among the parked cars. The vixen smirked as Joris circled her.

'Sweetheart.' He stretched leisurely before her. 'Honeydew. Perhaps you misheard. I'm the best suitor you'll have. Anything you want. You ever dreamed of a mountain of scraps? There's overflowing skips in the Old City. I can show you more food than you've ever seen in your life!' He sauntered back and forth, fully in his element now. 'You want to be safe and cosy? Come visit my bakery! They always keep the ovens warm there. Fancy running under the stars with nobody to catch you? Come with me! We'll go anywhere you want!' He hopped up onto a car bonnet. 'All the humans are cooped up inside like chickens now. We're kings of the roost here!'

The vixen just smiled. 'Or queens.'

Joris winced. 'Or queens, yeah. Sorry.' He cocked his head expectantly. 'Well? How about it?'

She laughed. 'Nah. Thanks again, but I'm fine. This here's my liddle patch. Nowhere else I'd rather be.'

'Oh.' *Think, you idiot, improvise!* Joris hopped down and began to circle. 'Perhaps a mate to warm your lonely nights, then? You name it. Whatever you want.'

She shrugged. 'Like I said, thanks. But I'm fine.'

Joris frowned. 'I don't understand. All the other foxes I've met over the seasons, they're all missing something. A fancy den. Plenty of food. A gorgeous vixen to share their bed – not that you'd want *that*, of course . . .'

She smiled. 'I might. You shouldn't just assume what others want. Oh, and don't call me honeydew, or sweetheart, or any more silly things. My name's Chekka.'

'Oh.' Joris hung his head, his brush trailing between his legs. 'You wanted a beautiful vixen, then? I'm so awfully sorry. I didn't realise.' He turned to leave.

'Stop,' she said. 'Just . . . just wait. Please.'

He looked back as Chekka trotted to his side. Her eyes were gentle. 'You always feel the need to impress, huh?'

'I . . .' he hung his head. *What in seven seasons is wrong with you, idiot? Where's that charming confident fox the ladies all swoon over?* '. . . I don't know.'

She turned her head, nose twitching. 'Hey, you hungry? Must be famished after all that talk. Fancy hunting some rats?'

'Uh . . .' Actually, now she came to mention it, he *was* rather hungry. 'Do you, erm . . . know where they hide?'

'Sure!' She darted away with a flick of her brush. 'Race you there!'

They dashed across the slumbering street, Chekka bounding ahead as she weaved through the parked cars like a tongue of fire. Joris hurried after her tinkling laughter. Both foxes scampered through the wet streets, lamplight splintering the puddles into shards of silver as they passed.

Soon they emerged onto the Thames foreshore, a black tunnel yawning before them. Chekka padded into the darkness. 'C'mon, then!'

Joris hesitated before the entrance. 'I don't know . . .'

She turned to grin back at him. 'Aww, what's the matter? You scared of the dark?'

'No, I . . .' *Crushing stone above. Only one way out. Suffocating walls pressing in on all sides. Not going in there – can't make me –*

'Hey.' Chekka trotted back alongside him,

nuzzling beneath his chin. 'We don't have to. Not if you don't want. It's okay.'

Focus, you idiot. It's just a tunnel. It ends. Eventually.

He stared at his paws, forcing the words out through gritted teeth. 'I want to. I mean . . .' *Why is this so hard?*

He looked up.

'Help me. Please.'

A greasy floor thick with mud and grime. They pressed on, squelching through the muck. Water dripped from an outflow pipe choked with sludge. Green slime crawled down the walls. The hiss of water sloshing into hundreds of tunnels echoed all around them, a dull rumble that prickled Joris's hackles. A clammy draught of air made him shudder.

Cold – dark – wet – trapped –

'I'm right here,' Chekka assured him. Her green eyes were gentle. 'I ain't going anywhere.'

Ahead of them came the whisper of many paws, the shrill squeaks of timid rodents. Dozens of yellow eyes leered from the shadows. Joris arched his back and began to prowl. Big greasy rats sat up on their haunches and sniffed the air. Some scuttled away, squeaking with fright. Flushed full of bravado Joris chased after them, snapping and driving them before him. *This'll show her! I'm the bravest fox there is!*

'Joris, wait!' Chekka called after him. 'It's too risky! Stay together!'

'Rubbish!' he scoffed. 'C'mon! Easy pickings here. Let's have some fun!' The rats streamed through a rusty culvert, and Joris squeezed through the broken bars after his prey, bristling with triumph. He snatched up a rat, shook it and tossed the limp corpse away. The others scattered and ran.

One didn't.

It hunkered down on all fours and hissed at him, a scabby dark-furred brute with a scarred nose. Joris stared down at it, unease prickling his guts. This wasn't right. Most prey he hunted fled from him immediately, screaming as they desperately sought to escape in vain. They were always far smaller than him, and dumber, and frozen with blind terror anyway. He shook himself and launched forwards, jaws agape . . .

. . . and crunched only empty air.

Joris blinked. His prey wasn't there. He turned. The black rat had darted close underneath his paws. It nipped Joris under the chin and vanished. He spun around. The rat still wasn't there. Joris shook his head, lips peeled back in a snarl. Needle-sharp teeth sank into his brush. He twisted in confusion.

79

He'd spent his life crunching prey that tried to run away. But this prey stayed really close, far too close for him to get a good bite in. It didn't run off like normal prey should. This wasn't fair! Pain lanced through his forepaw. He yelped and whirled around, snapping nothing but darkness.

The rat bared its teeth and squealed with rage.

More rats poured in, clawing up Joris's legs and hanging off his back. He shook them off and tried to bite but they ran at him again. Joris trampled on rats; he was pricked all over by sharp wicked fangs; he crunched one through the spine but still it clung on, alive and angry. He pushed through rats down the tunnel but the pack rippled after him, squealing with bloodlust. Joris was surrounded, tangled in wriggling hairy bodies that scratched and bit and leapt; he sucked in a desperate lungful of sewer as the writhing flood swarmed over him.

'Help!' he yelped.

And Chekka's screech shattered the darkness.

Something leapt over Joris and suddenly the tunnel was full of rats, just rats, nothing more than terrified squeaking rats fighting to escape a furious, snarling, spitting vixen. Chekka clawed and bit and ripped and snapped; rats were bowled over as the russet shadow smashed them aside and streaked after the black rat. It screamed as Chekka leapt upon it. Pain crashed through a blur of water, darkness and slime. Claws pinned it in the muck; again it squealed but Chekka's fangs snapped shut, and the squeal was instantly cut off.

Joris untwisted with a snarl. He was free. His ears flattened. His eyes flashed blue fire.

He couldn't think. He didn't think. No more talk, no more flattery. Just feral savage instinct moved him now, right down deep in his roaring blood. He bared his teeth, for he was a fox and here were twitching squeaking things all around and so he did what he was born to do, what foxes always do best: he *pounced* . . .

In a few furious minutes it was all over. Joris uncurled, panting as he gazed over his carnage. The tunnel floor was littered with twitching bodies, shrill wails of retreating rats echoing from the shadows. Chekka trotted close to nose-nuzzle. 'You okay?'

Joris tottered forwards, wincing from a dozen ugly gashes. 'Agh. I've had worse.' He licked her cheek. 'Thanks for rescuing me.' He sank to the floor, groaning with relief as Chekka began cleaning his wounds. 'Reckon that's enough rats for supper, eh?'

She sniggered and nibbled his ear. 'All right, you crazy cub. *Now* I'm impressed.' She nudged a limp corpse towards him. 'C'mon, greedy guts. Dig in!'

Having eaten their fill they trotted back down the tunnel, the Thames glittering before them. Soon they emerged onto the moonlit foreshore, paws crunching the gravel as they moved up the beach. The chimney stacks of Battersea Power Station soared before them, cold and silent, for its fires had burned out long ago. Gulls wailed out over the river, and above them lay a velvet sky dusted with stars.

They padded up the broad stone stairs of Chelsea Bridge onto the Embankment, flitting through the shadows like wraiths. As they passed underneath the viaduct the Southern Line train thundered overhead, clattering north towards Victoria Station.

Chekka slipped through the rusty iron railings into Battersea Park, quickening her pace. 'C'mon. Got something to show you!' Her white-tagged brush swished through the gloom ahead as Joris followed, his paws crunching the wet leaves. A hedgehog cowered under its leaf mound as they passed by, while a family of frightened coots huddled in their nests. Moonrise silvered the Boating Lake, and among the reeds by the pedalo jetty Skagg the heron tucked his beak under a wing and slept, dining on dream eels.

Chekka halted before a gnarled oak, blushing back at him. 'Well . . . this is me.'

Gazing about him, Joris marvelled at the vixen's simple life. Her cosy den safe beneath the tangled roots. Late-night pickings from the nearby shops, all within easy distance. The delicious scent of chips made his mouth water.

Except . . .

'Your life's good,' Joris told her, 'but you've nobody to share it with. Don't you ever get lonely?'

Chekka gazed steadily back. 'No. Why would I?'

Joris stared at his paws. 'This ain't right,' he muttered. 'Animals always want things. Everyone's hungry for something more. A mate. Food. A warm shelter for cold winter nights.'

'Not me. I've already got everything I need, right here.'

'Then what do *I* do?'

Chekka thought for a moment. Then she brightened. 'Can you clear away those leaves outside? They're a real nuisance whenever it gets windy.'

Joris gawped at her. '*That's* what you want me around for?'

'Nope. Just something useful you could do while I fetch us dinner.' She turned and vanished into the bushes.

Joris swept the damp leaves behind the oak with his brush. Eventually Chekka reappeared, dragging a sodden carrier bag in her jaws. Dumping it before her entrance, she slumped to the ground with a huff.

Joris nuzzled her ear. 'Tired?'

Chekka licked his cheek. 'Nah, just sore. Fancy giving an old fleabag a rub-down?'

Joris smiled and crouched over her, kneading her shoulders with his paws as she sighed with relief.

She opened her eyes and gazed up at him.

'There's something I never asked . . . what about you? What do *you* want?'

Joris curled his brush around her, and she snuggled her head against his chest.

'It's okay,' he murmured. 'I'm good.'

9
FOX FIRES

'But I'm one of you! I wanna join in!'

'Clear off, Maggot-Breath! You're a thievin' trickster!'

Aiden hung his head, face burning as the other woodlanders left through the trees, chuckling amongst themselves. Not his fault that he was hungry. Winter crawled on, lemmings were easy to catch – how was he to know that Akeela had recently laid claim to them? Even if he *was* Pack Leader . . .

But no. Whenever some mischief or grievance was discovered, the woodlanders always turned their anger upon Aiden, blaming him for every misfortune. Their whispers hissed through the frozen pines, prickling him to the bone. *Thief. Cheat. Trickster. Liar.*

A cold damp nose nuzzled his flank; silky white fur tickled his belly. He sighed. 'Come to cheer me up, Holly?'

'Let 'em have their laughs,' the arctic fox muttered, curling around his legs. 'You *know* they don't mean it.'

Aiden scoffed. 'Oh yeah? Like that time Hazel finally found his acorns after they'd gone all mouldy, and thought I'd dug 'em up? Or when the rabbit warren got barred with icicles and – surprise, surprise – they said I'd pushed snow over it! Always pickin' on me 'cause it suits them . . .'

Holly licked his cheek. 'Just rumours 'n' hearsay, Aiden. Don't let 'em rile you up.'

He twisted away from her, fuming. 'Stupid flopears, the lot of 'em. What d'you *expect* if you sleep under an earth bank when it's snowing . . . that it'll all wash away come sunrise?'

'Aiden, wait—'

'No, Holly!' He hurried away into the trees. 'Nobody listens! They never do!'

'Akeela! What d'you see?'

The wolf peered into the gloom, tail swishing uneasily. 'Not sure.' The other animals clustered at the wood's edge, the frozen lake stretching before them.

A ghostly figure swept over the ice. Her cloak sparkled with a thousand glittering white jewels, swirling around her like the hissing midwinter wind. The animals watched as she danced over the lake; wherever her feet trod or her staff brushed the ice, a new pinprick of light shone.

Akeela prowled forwards, hackles raised. 'Who are you? What've you done to our lake?'

The figure smiled, her eyes warm and gentle. 'I have many names, but you know me as Mother Moon. I need your help.'

Orren the ram strode to the lake's edge, curved horns lowered warily. 'Oh, really? And why would we do that?'

The cloaked figure knelt onto the ice. 'I am not as strong as the mighty sun.' She waved her arm; the lake dimmed before their eyes. 'I wax and I wane, and you are cast into darkness.' She straightened up. 'But if you join me, you will strengthen the night, and people will sing of you for countless generations.'

Stormclaw the bear reared up to his full height. 'Oh yeah? Pull the other one!'

The figure merely sighed. Raised her staff.

And slammed it down.

WHOOSH! A wave of blinding light flooded out from her feet. The animals watched, entranced as a thousand myriad stars twinkled upon the ice, many of them joined in lines of gleaming white fire.

'Help me,' Mother Moon murmured, 'and you will accomplish wonders among the stars.'

The animals exchanged glances, slow dawning smiles all around the group.

'All right,' Stormclaw grunted. 'How do we help?'

Mother Moon swept her arm out over the ice. 'Come forwards and you'll see.'

A moment's pause; then Akeela padded out onto the frozen lake. The ice creaked and groaned, but held fast. Halting before a line of glittering lights, he tentatively pressed his paw down.

The others watched in amazement as a wave of glowing light rose about him; Akeela's eyes gleamed with green fire, and his fur glistened with silver. Breaking into a run he bounded into the night sky with a howl of joy, drifting up to the glimmering heavens above.

The others eagerly pressed forwards to each cluster of light; Stormclaw lumbered into the chilly air, his eyes sparkling diamonds against the inky blackness of his coat. Orren galloped into the night sky, his horns and hooves gleaming with gold. And with each new volunteer, a fresh trail of glittering stars hung in the heavens above.

Aiden hung back among the trees, his heart throbbing with yearning. Oh, what *fun* it would be to join them among the stars! How the other woodlanders would welcome him back!

'C'mon, Aiden!' Holly trotted out onto the lake. Her fur sparkled with silver, every strand of fur glittering with brilliant light. She streaked into the air with an eager yelp. 'It's magical, Aiden! Come join us!'

Aiden trotted onto the ice, peering down at the shining gems stretching before him. Spying a promising cluster of gleaming diamonds, he raced towards it, pressing his paws down with a triumphant bark.

Nothing happened.

Unease shivered through him. *What's going on? Why won't it work?*

There! Another array of glittering pinpricks only a few leaps away. He scampered towards it, crouched on his haunches and sprang high over his prize—

Bonk!

Aiden slid away across the ice, spreadeagled as he nursed his aching nose. *This ain't right . . . why aren't I worthy?*

Another desperate pounce, and another! Nothing. Just the cold soaking into his paws, and the vast lonely lake stretching before him. A shimmering star mocked him silently from every puddle. *No, no, no . . .* He curled his brush around himself, misery knotting his guts like brambles.

'What's wrong, little one?' Mother Moon stood over him.

Aiden bowed his head. 'I tried so hard, but I can't do it. I can't become a star like them. I just . . . I wanted to help light up the night sky like everyone else!' He raised his muzzle and whimpered in despair.

'My friend left me behind and I'm . . . lonely.'

A gentle hand on his head. He closed his eyes as Mother Moon scratched tenderly behind his ears.

'Well,' she murmured, 'whoever said you could only become a star?'

And she touched her staff to the tip of his nose.

A wave of soothing warmth washed over him. Heat flooded through him from whisker-tip to tail-tuft. *What's happening to me? Is this what it feels like?* He clenched his paws tight, claws prickling into his pads.

He opened his eyes. Mother Moon smiled before him. 'Feels good, doesn't it?' Dazed, he looked down. And stared at his paws.

They weren't touching the ground!

He was floating above the ice. Tentatively he paddled his legs through the air, and drifted forwards. *This is incredible! I'm . . . I'm flying!* He sank slowly to earth, awestruck and overwhelmed.

High among the stars Holly whirled around, chasing her tail with excitement. 'You flew, Aiden! You *flew!*'

Mother Moon smiled proudly up at him. 'Well go on, then . . . she's waiting for you!'

Blood rushing through his ears, Aiden kicked hard against the ground. Up, up he soared, wind rushing through his fur and his brush streaming out behind him. Spying a distant range of mountains, he bounded towards them as Holly whooped in admiration.

Aiden alighted on the nearest craggy peak, panting heavily as his breath fogged the air. Mother Moon floated up to join him. 'Wasn't that fun?'

Aiden grinned at her. 'But . . . why choose me?'

Her smile widened. 'Look behind you.'

He turned. And gasped.

A trail of shimmering stardust shone behind him, kissing the highest peaks like gossamer lace. Great tumbling waterfalls of jewelled light hung and trembled in the air, all the colours of the rainbow draped over the mountains. Sparkling emerald, dazzling diamond, rose-pink and swirling gold that flashed through the night. At their base a deep fiery crimson, like the heart of a raging forest inferno. Beautiful beyond imagining.

Aiden stared, awestruck as Mother Moon continued, 'This is your legacy. You were born to run. You won't shine among the stars – instead you will drape the night with glorious wonders.' She gestured up to where Holly scampered among the clouds. 'And do not fear. Although you cannot join her among the stars, you will run together, and at the end of every moonfall, she will *always* be waiting.'

Holly pranced with glee. 'C'mon, Aiden,' she called. 'Race you to the horizon!'

Aiden leapt upwards, streaking through the air as his brush left a winding stream of jewelled light in his wake. With a rush of fierce pride he knew he'd found his true purpose – this was easy, this was *wonderful!*

'Keep up, you old brushtail!' Holly giggled. 'Let's go!'

Aiden dashed after her, soaring through the clouds as he barked with joy. 'Second star to the right, Holly, and straight on until morning! Race you there!' He vanished into the night, running under the brilliant stars to where his beloved Holly was waiting for him.

And to this day, and forevermore . . . they are still running together.

10
ONE LAST RUN

Kyle raced through gorse under the shadow of Black Tor, the drizzle sheeting into his eyes. A frightened partridge whirred up from the brambles and the wind smacked it away. He raced over the moorland under churning grey cloud, the hounds' yelps echoing in his ears.

Lancer led the pack past Ford Farm, tracking his quarry's scent relentlessly among the bracken. Kyle slithered down the slope of prickling thistles into the riverside undergrowth. He could smell the hounds far behind; above the moan of the wind Lancer's baying filled the valley. Were they gaining on him? Slipping into the river he let the current sweep him down to the copse at White Bridge. The water would mask his trail.

For now.

The rain had lifted. Pushing deeper into the thicket he caught the musky stink of hare. His nose pulled him to the root tangle of a fallen oak smothered in moss. He peered into the gloom. Large rheumy eyes squinted back.

'So the pack *is* coming,' a voice quavered. 'Sometimes I can't tell if I'm dreaming or not.' A silver-furred hare with scarred ears raised his head.

Kyle trotted closer and sniffed. Once he might have swept in and savaged his prey in a heartbeat; now he felt only pity. 'What do they call you?'

'Bramwill Swiftpaw.' The ancient hare uncurled with a groan. 'Agh . . . this tapeworm's given me hell, so last night I ran with the storm and ended up here.'

'Where next?'

'The Star Place.' Bramwill smiled. 'I've run far enough. Still, to see eight glorious summers is a blessing.' His eyes creased with concern. 'Are the hounds pushing you?'

Kyle snorted. 'Seasons, no! They couldn't catch a blind earthworm on a straight road.'

'What about a sick old hare?' murmured Bramwill. 'Would they do for him?'

Kyle nipped a flea from his belly-fur. 'It ain't necessary. I could lead them round in circles until midnight and leave them chasing moonbeams.'

A distant clamour of howling far behind. They had regained his scent. Kyle sniffed the air. 'Half a mile off, d'you reckon?'

Bramwill's ragged ears twitched. 'Closer.'

Kyle frowned. 'There's no need for this. I could lay a false trail, lead 'em safely astray.'

Bramwill gazed steadily back. 'Would you deny me the Good Death?'

Kyle shivered. To be broken up under the pack's jaws when your strength finally deserted you . . . still, at least hounds were swift killers. Merciful, even, compared with Man-filth's cruel devices. The slow strangling from wire snares. The clawing agony from poison bait. The steel traps that left you crippled and helpless, awaiting a hail of buckshot or a crowbar to split your skull . . .

He shook his head. 'Never, friend.'

'No more words, then,' Bramwill sighed and creaked upright, stretching his scrawny limbs. 'One last run, eh?'

Predator and prey touched noses. 'See you in the golden fields one day,' Kyle said.

Bramwill smiled. 'Swear you won't chase me, brushtail?'

Kyle grinned back. 'No promises, longears.' He turned and left the old runner to his destiny. The hounds echoed again.

Bramwill breathed in deep and hopped out from the shelter of the trees. Lifting his face to the open sky he closed his eyes. High above a lark was singing.

Though I may die,
the grass will grow,
the sun will shine,
the stream will flow.

Bramwill recalled the first time his mother had chanted the prayer in their cosy nest beneath the ash saplings. His heart ached at the memory, the warm snuffling bodies of his leveret brothers and sisters as they nuzzled close to suckle. Long years had passed since then; seven cruel winters, eight wonderful summers among the buttercups. In the golden years of his prime he could run like the wind, outbox all rivals and leave dogs gasping in his dust.

But that was then.

Now he was a weary veteran of a hundred chases; years of defending his territory had taken their toll. Age had stiffened his bones like hoarfrost and sapped the strength from his limbs. He grimaced at every gnawing pain, yet the pursuing hounds were fresh and eager. No chance of outpacing them over open moorland.

But I can try.

He clenched his jaw. And ran on.

Though I may lose
this body of mine,
the grass will grow,
and the stars will shine.

His coat was sodden with sweat, yet the hot ache in his stomach had melted away and he ran with the swift suppleness of a young buck. Purple waves of heather rose and fell beneath his galloping paws, while his past fell behind him and vanished into mist.

He glanced back. The hounds were crashing through the bracken, baying ferociously. Lancer was way out in front, his jaws agape and slobbering with bloodlust as he streaked ahead.

They were closing in.

Bramwill bounded around the southern slope of Black Tor, skidding over the rough scree. Grit sprayed everywhere as he stumbled onto firmer heathland. Despair curled its icy claws through him; for the first time he realised just how much his death meant to these dogs – and to their owner. Could they really have hated him so much over the years? Now, for the first time, he had no plans, no strategy left. His long weary years of toil and bitter experience had come to naught. He'd tried everything and yet here they still remained, relentless and bloodthirsty, eager to rip his life away.

Remorse shivered through him; once the hounds caught him it would be finished. He would never again taste the succulent dandelions, nor savour each dewdrop kissed by the dawn. The burning rush of triumph as he towered over a beaten rival. The tender warmth of a doe's love. The tinkling music of twilight birdsong.

He hardened his heart, steely resolve flooding through his limbs.

*Dying be damned . . . I want to **live**!*

Behind him Lancer bellowed. Bramwill gave a wild laugh.

*Fancy a chase, you slime-brained arse-sniffer? You can bloody well **try**.*

It was as if the long seasons had fallen away from the old hare; strength coursed through his veins like wildfire. He hurtled over the moor and tore down into the valley, up the slope towards the crooked shadow of Shelstone Tor. Now he was running for his very life itself, and at a breathtaking speed he had never touched before, not even in the glory days of his youth. This was easy . . . this was *wonderful!*

Bramwill never saw the stray root that tripped him. One moment, he was streaking over the mossy boulders of Meldon Down, the hounds' roaring growing fainter in his ears and victory soaring in his heart; the next, lancing pain shot through his forepad and the ground was hurtling up to meet him. He tumbled ears-over-bobtail, air punched from his lungs as he crashed into the brush.

The jumble of rocks loomed before him. Shelter. Safety. Wheezing for breath, he limped into the shadows, wincing at every jolting ache in his limbs.

A sheer wall of granite towered above him. Nowhere to run. Nowhere to hide.

A low rumbling growl behind him. Lancer slunk around the boulder, drool dripping from his bared jaws. Bramwill set his back to the rock – his only defence – and lurched up onto his hindlegs, paws clenched.

Stand and fight then . . . go out in a blaze of thunder!

Lancer howled and lunged. Bramwill sprang to meet him, lashing out furiously with his forepaws. Once! Twice! Digging his claws deep into Bramwill's back, Lancer howled with triumph, swiftly followed by a yelp of pain as Bramwill's teeth sank deep into his leg. Kicking out savagely Bramwill scored two vicious blows to Lancer's ribs, then gasped as Lancer's claws raked across his face. They broke apart, both sorely wounded. Then Bramwill shook the blood from his eyes, and with a bellow of rage he charged the hound.

They smashed together; kicking, scratching, gouging and snapping, both fighters rolled over and over in a shower of flying earth. Lancer wriggled free first, leaving Bramwill prone upon the ground. Growling with triumph he backed away, licking his stinging wounds.

Then Bramwill stirred.

Shaking himself he staggered upright, breathing raggedly. Lancer snorted in disbelief, baring his fangs as he pawed the earth. Bramwill grinned through a mouthful of blood. 'C'mon, you ugly brute . . . I'm right here!'

With a wild howl the hound plunged in—

A blur of russet lightning slammed into him, bowling him sideways with a screech.

Kyle! Bramwill watched in dazed amazement as the fox prowled protectively before his battered body, hackles raised, teeth bared, his golden eyes blazing. There was coiled menace in every line of Kyle's bristling fur, emanating an implacable ferocity as palpable as scorching heat.

'You . . . you came back!' he gasped.

'Couldn't let you have all the fun, could I?' Kyle

growled, eyes fixed on the fallen hound. Lancer uncurled, snarling. Kyle cocked his leg and sprinkled the earth.

Challenge accepted!

Lancer scrabbled upright and leapt, howling with rage. Kyle met him mid-leap. They fought like savage beasts in a shower of dust and torn grass, fangs snapping, claws raking, limbs kicking furiously. Twisting free Lancer flung himself upon the fox. Kyle yelled as Lancer's teeth sank deep into his shoulder—

Bramwill lurched upright. His paws were deadened from a dozen ragged wounds, but his blood was up and his jaws were strong. Gathering all his remaining strength he hurled himself upon Lancer, sinking his incisors deep into the hound's leg and biting it savagely to the bone.

Lancer writhed in the dust, wailing with anguish. A flailing hindpaw struck Bramwill's face yet he clung on grimly. Seizing his chance Kyle lunged for Lancer's throat. The hound's eyes bulged as Kyle's teeth crushed his windpipe.

They sank to the earth, jaws locked as the dust billowed about them. Lancer lashed about in mad panic, snuffling and choking. His mouth full of flesh and fur, Kyle kept hold. He couldn't break his enemy's neck like a rabbit's – Lancer was far too heavy – but if he could just hang on . . .

Lancer's air finally ran out. His eyes rolled back into their sockets and his dead weight dragged Kyle down. The fox opened his jaws; Lancer's head thumped limply into the dirt. Bramwill released his grip, gazing down at Lancer's lifeless body.

He swayed. Blinked at Kyle. 'Nasty business, eh . . . oh, corks!' Then his legs buckled beneath him and he collapsed.

Kyle hurried to his side. 'Hang in there, Bramwill! C'mon now. I've got you, mate!' Peering over Bramwill's shoulder, he gasped in horror at the long ripping wounds down Bramwill's back.

The ancient hare gave a wheezing chuckle. 'Sneaky rotter got a cheap shot in. Wasn't very sportin' of him, was it?'

Kyle licked his wizened brow, fixing a brave smile on his face. 'Shhh. Rest now. You've earned it. Be right as rain in no time!'

Bramwill shook his head and smiled weakly. 'That brute got me good. At least I outlived him.' He shuddered and blinked, trying to focus. 'Funny . . . I'm so very tired. Jolly cold!' He coughed raggedly. 'Do me one last favour, Kyle.'

Hot tears glistened in Kyle's eyes. 'Anything, mate. You name it.'

Bramwill lay back, eyes clouding over. 'See me

out, eh? Take whatever you need from me, but don't leave me for the scavengers, wot! A feast for the crows? Not bloody likely!' He clutched Kyle's paw. 'You'll make it quick?'

Kyle curled around him, his thick fur soothing Bramwill's battered bones. 'On my honour, you old battler. Easier than falling asleep.'

'Every sunset . . .' the grizzled hare gazed up at Kyle, '. . . remember me, won't you?' His eyelids flickered one last time, then they closed. For ever. His head lolled back, baring his throat.

Kyle bowed his head.

'I will.'

Bramwill was free. Beyond the black silence of Kyle's jaws the meadows of endless grass and eternal summer moonlight opened up to welcome him. The weary weight of his long seasons fell away, and each star-kissed blade of grass sparkled as he ran on towards the golden sunrise.

Thus passed Bramwill Swiftpaw, a fighter to the bitter end.

Kyle gazed down at the ancient hare. Bramwill lay not in peaceful sleep; he looked as if he had died in battle, yet that his fight had been victorious.

Offering up a silent prayer to the heavens, Kyle accepted the old warrior's final gift to him. With deft slashes of his foreclaws, he opened Bramwill's body and began to feed. It was his first meal since dawn, and he was hungry. The brave hare's flesh and blood would nourish Kyle through the night and into a new day.

The sun was setting as Kyle finished his meal. After gathering the bone fragments into a neat heap, he began to dig.

A feast for the crows? Not on his watch.

He dug down. Down. A deep trench in the dry earth, safely beyond the reach of carrion crows and bone-pickers. Sweeping the bones down into the darkness, Kyle began to fill the hole. A kestrel hovered weightless high above, then dropped like a stone behind the clitter of rocks. Kyle laboured on. His last vow to a noble fighter.

Eventually the grave was finished, a mound of fresh soil among the whispering tussocks. Kyle sat back on his haunches. Soon Bramwill's body would be nourishing a dozen different forms of life. He lifted his muzzle and howled to the sunset.

'Rest well, old warrior,' he whispered. And trotted away over the hill.

He thought he saw a shadow from the corner of his eye; a flicker of silver fur, an echo of husky laughter. But when he turned there was nothing there.

Oh well. He'd see his old friend again eventually.

Everyone would, in the end.

In the meantime, he had all the sunsets in the world.

11
FUR AND FANG

Logan the otter streamed through the tangled undergrowth, the sour reek of sweat and petrol flooding his nostrils. 'Quick!' he barked as chittering squirrels fled before him. 'Run! Man's coming!'

On the bridge the trapper lounged against his jeep, twelve-bore over his shoulder as he drained his hip flask. The pale lurcher strained at his leash, blood madness churning behind his eyes. The trees rustled above him, singing to him to reap their red harvest, eager for their share of meat. 'We're lonely, Ripper,' they'd whisper to him. 'Send us sheep, lambs, rabbits and foxes. Kill 'em quick and they come play with us.' He loved nothing better than basking in the rabbits' bleating screams as they fled from him in glorious panic. His kingdom was full of victims who awaited his coming and welcomed his savage embrace. 'Kill-kill-kill,' he'd croon to himself as the hot blood flowed, savouring the lightheaded bliss as he'd rip the life from his prey. 'All beasts get chopped, get sent to trees. And trees whisper "Good dog, Ripper", and Ripper get best place by fireside.' He whined and tugged at the leash.

'Can 'e smell fox, boy?' the trapper grinned. 'Go get 'im! Go on – good dog. Good Ripper!' He unclipped the leash; Ripper tore off through the undergrowth, blindly smashing through bracken and primroses. The trapper's whistle sliced through the summer afternoon.

The musky scent of fox washed over Logan as he approached the den. Golden eyes gleamed. A tawny vixen padded out of the darkness, two cubs cowering behind her. She bared her teeth at the interloper: another crafty weasel come to play tricks on her?

'Quickly!' he urged. 'We gotta go! How many cubs you got?'

'Two,' she growled, hackles raised. 'But what—'

'One each, and *hurry*,' Logan snapped. 'The trapper's coming. His lurcher too. *Right now*.'

She sneered. 'And I s'pose the river told ya that, water weasel?'

He snorted. 'Survivin' for eight winters told me.

C'mon!' Before she could snarl he grabbed the nearest cub by the scruff of her neck and dashed into the trees.

They ran through the beech saplings and wriggled under the hedge. The cub yelped as a twig scraped her nose. Logan tightened his grip and hurried down the grassy slope behind the churning watermill. Across the black-tarred road that scorched his pads, around the crumbled drystone wall, through the rotting undergrowth past the drooping willow, plunging into scratchy ferns at the water's edge. A lanky heron flapped clumsily downriver. A wren shrilled and darted across the water.

Logan's holt entrance yawned before them, overshadowed by a towering oak. A warren of a dozen hidden tunnels and boltholes to safety. Logan crept into the darkness, past the mass of gnarled roots guarding the passageway. Down into the sandy hollow carpeted with straw where his three pups tumbled over each other, mewing with joy at their father's safe return. Gail's whiskered face chittered at him. 'What in Hellsteeth's going on?'

Logan lowered his wriggling cargo. 'Trapper's coming. Lurcher too.' His pups huddled together, the two fox cubs crawling over to join them. The stale air stank with their fear.

A muffled scrabbling above them. The distant hollers of the trapper: 'Get down there, Ripper! In! In! Chase 'em out!'

Logan slunk to the tunnel mouth. 'Wait here,' he growled. 'Just keep your cubs quiet, all right?'

The vixen puffed out her chest proudly. 'Her name's *Neera*. And this is Jemi, my son. I'm Sonya.'

Logan rolled his eyes. 'Whatever. That lurcher ain't comin' in here. I'll see 'im off.'

'How?' Sonya asked. 'He's a monster! Got great long legs and a huge mouth!'

Logan bared his teeth in a feral grin. 'So's the heron.' Gail sniggered.

Logan crept up the passageway, past the mass of gnarled oak roots curling into the tunnel. The tunnel mouth darkened as Ripper jabbed his pointed muzzle inside, fangs snapping eagerly. Logan thumped his rudder against the floor, his rank fur stench wafting up to flood Ripper's nostrils, driving him into a blood-frenzy.

That's it. Logan thought. *Come on, Scat-eater. Come get me!* He squirmed down into the gloom, worming his way back until his heavy tail brushed the knotted roots. Inching backwards he braced his webbed feet against them, sunk into the darkness like a coiled viper.

Waiting.

The lurcher howled as he gulped the rank stink of otter. He clawed into the tunnel, frantic to *bite-rip-tear-maim*. Soil showered down around him as he wriggled deeper, claws gashing the earthen walls. 'Kill-kill-kill,' the trees whispered to him as he ploughed into the musty blackness. Deeper. Deeper.

Logan waited.

Just a bit further . . . come on . . .

Ripper squeezed forwards. Walls pressing in around him. Maddened with bloodlust he crawled into the darkness, chasing his prey. Deeper. Deeper.

And jerked to a halt.

The earth was crushing his ribs. His bony frame squeezed tight between two rocky spurs. His long legs – perfect for running down prey over open ground – now pinned him against the roof. Unable to kneel. Nowhere to turn. He was wedged fast in the narrow tunnel, the damp stench of earth flooding his senses, jaws snapping on empty darkness. Trapped. Helpless. Fear curled its claws through him. Maybe this animal was . . .

And Logan struck!

Surging out of the darkness, he crashed into Ripper like a battering ram, smashing the breath from his lungs and crunching his left forepaw.

110

Ripper squealed and twisted in desperation, struggling to wriggle free. But the cramped tunnel hampered his turning and the smothering darkness was alive with a writhing, snarling, hissing fury that drowned his senses in icy dread. He scrabbled back, cracking his head on the roof. Soil showered down on him. Part of the wall crumbled inwards – space! Then Logan's claws viciously raked his soft underbelly, ripping, tearing, pain searing through him. Blind and terrified Ripper lashed out, fangs latching deep into sodden neck-scruff. But Logan wrenched free, thwacking away at Ripper's gashed belly with his heavy rudder.

Once! Twice! Thrice!

Battered and whimpering Ripper fell back, bleeding from a dozen wounds as the otter streamed past him into the widened tunnel. The choking stink of mustelid flooded his nostrils and he gave chase up the tunnel, baying with vengeance.

Come on, Logan willed him on. *That's it. Follow me, you great blundering idiot. I'm right here!*

Deep underground in the otters' hollow, Neera squeaked and nuzzled into her mother's belly. Sonya curled around her, soothing her whimpers with gentle licks as Jemi shrank against them, trembling. Gail chittered in reassurance as her pups huddled close. The distant echo of Ripper's bloodthirsty wail dribbled down the tunnel.

'What now?' Sonya breathed.

Gail brushed noses with her. 'Now we wait.'

Safe. For the moment.

Logan streaked over the dewy grass like a wraith, smearing his musky scent with his rudder and his water-sleeked coat. Ripper raged behind him, snarling in his blood-crazed desire to rip this filthy challenger limb from limb. Logan flowed over the mass of tangled roots, dribbling scat in his wake to lead the maddened lurcher onward.

The shotgun roared; the air hissed above him as wood splinters rained down. A screaming pheasant exploded out of the bracken. He darted left, pads crackling the fallen leaves as Ripper struggled through the thorny brambles behind. Over the ridge, on to the wizened oak choked with ivy overlooking the river. He paused to douse the trunk with his scent. Turning back, he hissed in defiance. An otter in his element – let them hunt him now! Gliding over the riverbank, he melted into the water.

Ripper crested the ridge and skidded to a halt, eyes blazing at his quarry taunting him mid-river. Chevrons of water rippled outward as Logan followed the current, the bloodthirsty lurcher scrambling through the undergrowth after him.

Slipping underwater, he dimly heard Ripper's muffled barks.

Draw him out. The hunter who loses his advantage loses his life.

He surfaced to gaze at Ripper. The lurcher's snout wrinkled in a snarl.

Logan bared his teeth and yickered with scorn.

It was the final straw. Ripper howled and charged, spraying pebbles as he crashed into the shallows. Bloodlust boiled through his skull. How his master would love him and feed him the tasty scraps off his plate, and the trees would whisper sweet lullabies. Kill the otter, kill the fox, kill his prey. Kill-kill-kill.

Jungled in swaying reeds, Logan waited. His sunken kingdom sprawled about him, a rippling forest of shimmering emerald. Last year's rotting leaves drowned in mud.

The glimmering surface far above, sliced through with sunlight. The muffled thrashing of Ripper's paws as he blundered through the water.

Now!

Logan launched upwards, crashing into Ripper with staggering force and dragging him down into the grey murkiness. Ripper gulped desperately for air, but only swallowed water. The surface boiled in a welter of churning water, ragged grey fur and streaks of black blood. A wordless wail of terror burst from Ripper's lips, the ravenous land-hunter suddenly trapped in a black icy airless void. Logan felt a venomous thrill scorch through him.

Welcome to my world, Scat-eater!

His jaws clamped tight on Ripper's hindleg, crunching it savagely through to the bone. The lurcher flailed in panic, claws raking feebly across Logan's muzzle as he twisted and writhed. *Stupid mutt*, Logan thought. *You're just burning air. And you ain't getting more. Trust me*. He tightened his grip, jaws locked around Ripper's leg as he dragged them down. Deeper. Deeper. A remorseless rhythm that growled *more*, *more*, *more*. They sank down together, a wriggling mass of flailing limbs and swirling bubbles. Down. Down. Down into the murky green gloom. A forest of swaying weed loomed below, clouds of brown silt billowing around them. Ripper was screaming now, bubbles rushing from his mouth in a frenzied torrent. An iron band crushing his skull.

Finally, his last living breath leaked out of his starving lungs. And the water poured in.

The sunlight flashed like a shoal of silver fish high above. And dimmed.

And vanished.

Ripper sank into the murky depths. His legs no

longer twitched. His wide eyes stared into nothingness, and Logan swam off leaving a trail of rising bubbles.

Sonya and Gail crouched in the musky hollow, their young curled around them. Suddenly a shadow darkened the tunnel entrance. Larger. Larger. The infants shrank together, whimpering. Sonya bared her teeth. Gail bristled, hackles raised . . .

Logan's low whistle echoed through the hollow. The otter slunk out of the gloom, grinning as his pups squirmed over him with joyful squeaks.

'We're safe,' he rumbled.

Gail nuzzled against him. 'Where's the mutt?'

'Feeding the fishes,' Logan smirked. Sonya nudged her cubs forwards with her snout.

'Remember your manners,' she prompted. 'Thank the brave hunter who kept you safe.' Neera wobbled forwards on shaky legs to lick Logan's muzzle.

'Fank you,' she mumbled shyly. 'My name's—'

'Neera,' Logan brushed noses with her, his tickling whiskers making her giggle. 'Your mum told me. Pleased to meet you, miss.'

12
WINTER'S BITE

Deep in her musty holt, Kayla the otter uncurled on her litter of twigs to nuzzle her mewling pup, who squirmed close eager for milk. 'Hush, Finn. Your father'll be home soon.' Hunger's claws raked her belly as she soothed Finn's squeaking with gentle licks.

Her mate's low whistle echoed through the hollow; Kayla's heart leapt as Theo slunk into the birthing chamber with a limp mouse in his jaws.

'Hey, catkin,' she grinned. 'Couldn't've brought any plump ducks along with you?'

Theo set his offering down and tenderly licked her brow. 'Sorry, rosebud. The poacher wasn't takin' requests. Ellak already snagged one from his coop this morning.'

Kayla sniggered. 'Stubborn as an old badger, that rascal. He'll get himself caught in a wire one o' these days.' She crunched his gift down eagerly but the small gnawer of willow bark was barely a morsel, a scant thimbleful of fur and bone.

Her stomach gurgled; Theo buried his muzzle into her shoulder with a chuckle. 'Still peckish, famine chops?'

Kayla rolled her eyes. 'I'm wasting away here. Nothing but skin and bone!' She pouted up at him. 'Your son's a real whiner too!'

Theo smirked. 'Wonder where he gets that from?'

Kayla nipped his flank. 'Oh, harr harr. Very funny, ya great pudden riverdog!' She groaned with relief as Theo curled around them both, nuzzling into his warmth as he licked her cheek. They gazed down with fond smiles as their pup rolled onto his back, pawing the air.

'Young rascal wants feedin' up,' Kayla grinned. 'Doesn't want to be kept waiting, do ya, sonny?'

From his mother's belly Finn gave a rough squeak. Theo nodded solemnly. 'Right you are, milord. Dinner's on its way.'

He trotted back to the surface, the tunnel echoing with Kayla's chittering laughter.

The North Wind hissed through the valley, swirling over hillocks and whispering into sunken hollows. It shivered the mace-heads in the rustling marsh as

Krogg the heron stood sentinel, scanning the torpid water for the faintest glitter of fish. He stalked gravely into the shallows, feathers ruffled against the winter's chill as a skewered rat warmed his belly. He bent low, peering. Speared with a swift lunge. Gulped only water. The Arctic chill swept over hill and dale, moaning through the frozen forest as it hung icicles from branches and boltholes. A thick shroud of snow choked the wilted shrubs, diamond dust draped over crinkled ferns like gossamer lace. Corvo the raven settled on a frost-jewelled branch, his croaks rattling against the fogged cottage window.

Jackson jerked up from his armchair with a groan, the acid stew of last night's cider, cheese and pickles gurgling in his throat. 'Urgh – Jesus!' That same bloody nightmare, Rifleman Billy Jackson of the Royal Norfolks sprawled in the riverbank's sucking mud as a wounded swan flapped feebly alongside him, its tripe spilled out by shrapnel. All day the stench of death had smothered his nose until nightfall, when two otters melted out of the darkness. The lame swan gasping and whimpering as they swarmed over it like writhing eels, lips peeled back on crimson froth. The vast snowy wings had flapped, and twitched, and stilled, there on that riverbank in France. 'Christ!' Rifleman

Jackson had thought. 'Them buggers'll be eatin' me next!' He'd rasped curses at the otters but still they gnawed, crunching and snapping loud in his ears until he awoke in the field hospital.

Lurching to the kitchen window he belched and shook his head, gulping blessed lungfuls of icy air as he waited for the nausea to sink. The sightless masks of two grizzled dog foxes glared down from the wall alongside three weasel corpses snarling in death. The poacher stared out into the hazy white shroud, the thunder of eighteen-pounders receding into a past that refused to die.

'Craarck,' Corvo croaked. 'Craarck-craarck.'

Jackson winced, sweat beading his brow. He rammed home the shells and thumbed back the hammers. 'Shuddup!' The window creaked open, weak grey light dribbling in. The shotgun clapped twice. Corvo fluttered to earth unhurt, the woods echoing with his bawdy chuckles. 'Bloody hell, Bill,' Corporal Smith grimaced. 'You want every Kraut in Flanders knowin' we're 'ere?' Smacking a hand to his clammy forehead Jackson squinted at the silent duckhouse.

Shouldering open the door, he staggered back with a hoarse cry. 'Jesus wept!' His three prize mallards huddled in their gloomy stalls, the fourth cubicle drowned in a mess of bloody feathers.

Jackson reeled away, fists clenched in his hair as he howled at the watery sun.

There! In the churned mud amid the triple-toed prints of crows and the narrow pads of foxes: the broad five-clawed trace of an otter.

'Old Blackie,' he snarled, blood hissing through his ears. His sworn enemy, the cunning foe who'd already slipped his snares twice this week, taunting him with a dribble of black slime. The otter's prints trailed through the snow and vanished through the hole in the fence. Towards the marshes.

'You ain't gettin' me, boyo.' Fumbling his Wellington boots on, Jackson stuffed shells into his pockets and stormed off towards the wetland. The naked trees crowded around him, whispering.

Theo pattered over the frozen lake, his pads crunching the frail shell as he shivered the icicled reeds in his wake, nose twitching at every scent. The frosty air was alive with the damp stink of rotting leaves and shrivelled moss, and fieldfares flashed among the leafless trees. Passing by the frost-rimmed mouth of Ellak's den Theo whistled hello, but the fox dozed deep underground, deaf to the frozen world above. No more hunting today – not with a plump mallard warming his belly!

Loping through the snow, Theo spied Brock the

old boar badger grubbing for worms and barked a greeting, but Brock grunted, 'Hmph . . . company!' and trundled into the woods.

Cresting the ridge Theo flowed downhill on his belly, snow tickling his whiskers as he whooped in play. A marsh harrier trilled in reply from the hollow where it gorged on a vole's steaming carcass, and the rowans overlooking the marsh were laden with waxwings. Snaking through the reeds Theo emerged, craning up on his haunches to peer into the marsh. Krogg's head bobbed at his feeding spot, beak lancing as he greedied on a steaming trout that had floundered on the riverbank. Crystals glittered on its scales as the heron jabbed again and again.

The brackish marsh water scarcely rippled as Jackson waded through the broken reeds, his breath fogging the air.

Theo sank onto all fours and crawled towards Krogg. The sheet whined and creaked then *boom*! a thin blue crack scuttled out from his broad pads. Water spurted. He flinched back, lowered his paw gingerly. Another hairline fissure. He wormed forwards. Inch by inch.

Krogg lifted his beak from his plump prize. Black eyes slithered over the whispering marshland. Something was close . . .

Theo barrelled out of the reeds with a hiss, hackles bristling. Krogg flapped clumsily downriver, croaking his displeasure. The trout's pink flesh glistened in the sunshine. Belly growling with hunger, Theo bent low to feed.

Click.

He flung himself sideways as the shotgun roared. Buckshot hissed past his head, spattering his face with icy shards. Whirling around he yickered with scorn.

'Black bastard!' Jackson snarled, fumbling with his cartridges. 'Stay still!' Theo streaked out onto the frozen lake, ice pitching and creaking beneath him. Behind him Jackson fought to steady the gun. His eyes watered. His hands shook. But Theo was a large target, the only dark shadow in the desolate white emptiness.

Jackson squeezed the trigger. Pain sliced across Theo's flank as the pellets bit deep. He tumbled over, sprawled out and defenceless.

Jackson's breath hitched. Bullseye! The moorhen screamed; the trench whistle shrilled. 'Over the top, lads!' Sergeant Evans called. Jackson felt a venomous thrill scorch through him – one good clubbing swing with the shotgun and he'd have Blackie's pelt for sure. He'd go to the White Inn and be crucified behind the bar above the brandy bottles. Caught by Billy Jackson – better glory than having your name on the village cenotaph.

Better to finish it up close. Let his enemy know who beat him. Savour the light fading from his eyes.

He stepped onto the ice. The sheet whined and groaned and splintered.

But it held. Mist curled like steam around him as he stomped forwards. The watery sun hung like a flickering flare in the west. The creaks and groans of frozen trees melted into the sharp crackle of rifle fire. He was marching through no man's land as the icy chill stung his cheeks. Khaki shadows either side of him, rippling like a windswept field of barley under the chatter of machine guns. Bodies jerking and shuddering on the wire as the bullets smashed deep. 'On, boys. On!' Captain Turner barked.

Theo writhed helplessly on the ice, teeth gritted against the grinding pain. *I won't scream*, he silently vowed. *Not for this maggot-filth.*

The ice whined and cracked under Jackson's boots. Another step. And another. Closer. Closer.

Theo glared in defiance as Jackson loomed over his injured enemy. 'Nein, Kamarad!' the German soldier had pleaded, but the bayonet was deaf. In, grunt. Out, grunt.

'Who's laughin' now?' the poacher smirked. Cracks spiderwebbed around his boots. Theo bared his teeth . . .

. . . and smashed his rudder down onto the ice.

CRACK!

The ground splintered; Jackson stumbled forwards as his feet lurched beneath him. 'Fuckin' 'ell!' The ice yawned wide as the cold clawed up his shins, his legs, his calves. He flailed desperately for solid ice but his boots were sinking, sinking. Then his world tilted and he was falling, falling, falling. 'Get outta the mud, Bill,' Private Allen muttered. 'Quit lazin' about, mate. The Krauts are comin'!'

The lake folded him into its icy embrace, pouring into his eyes, his ears, his mouth. His fists hammered feebly against the thick icy roof, but all the while he was sinking, choking, drowning, his sodden clothes dragging him down.

Down.

Down.

The lake was silent. Chunks of ice bobbed, and rippled, and stilled again. Before the last crashing echoes had died away Theo was gone, vanished on the mist like a silent moon shadow.

With Krogg's frozen trout safe in his jaws.

13
FREEDOM IN EXILE

Brockthorn the badger prowled before his sett. 'Why should *I* leave,' he muttered, 'just because some uppity twigheads want to be closer to the lake?'

'Rubbish!' Rufus snorted. 'You can dig out a bigger home in a day or two.' He tilted his antlers towards the small clan of badgers gathered at the woodland edge. 'Besides, all your friends moved along without a fuss. What's *your* problem here?'

Brockthorn bristled. 'It's my home! They only went because *you* told them a heap of scat about how great the cemetery was.'

Rufus scuffed a hoof among the fallen leaves. 'But the cemetery's perfectly fine. There's trees all around and far more rats for you to eat.'

Brockthorn rolled his eyes. 'Because it's right alongside the town! There's people everywhere! It's not like the park's too cramped here for all of us.

You just don't want to share the best spots, do you?'

'Don't be ridiculous,' Rufus sneered.

The spring sunset was awash with pink, the lake glittering as fish gulped water boatmen on the surface. Frogs clambered up the rocks to bask in the warm dusk, licking flies from the air. Brockthorn had learned to hunt here, his father teaching him to lie low in the grass and stalk the slowest, fattest frogs.

He slumped back on his haunches, dark eyes narrowed. 'If the cemetery's so stinking great, why don't the deer move *there*?'

The stag towered over him. 'Don't be stupid. We need to be near fresh water. Can you imagine having to trek back and forth every day, out in the open like that? Being exposed all the time?'

'Oh, but it's *fine* for us?' Brockthorn grunted.

'Exactly,' Rufus sighed. 'Look, we're different animals with different needs. Foxes, rabbits, moles, badgers – you're all fine nearer the town. You're underground all day and you can use the lake at night, anyway. We deer need shelter, more grass and open space to run. Our wood's getting much too crowded and our own pond's far too small.'

Brockthorn bared his teeth. 'Rat scat! You just think you're so much better than us. Always have. You think you can push everyone in this park around. Or bribe them onto your side. Now you come over here all: "Ooh! We fancy a bit of this lake actually, so clear out of the way or get an antler up the arse", hm? Am I wrong?'

'You'd best be quiet, *vermin*,' Rufus rumbled. 'You know why we're in charge. You think any old animal can organise Park Watch? Keep you all safe? This park's *nothing* without us.'

'It was perfectly fine before *you* became Head Stag,' Brockthorn growled.

Rufus's lip curled. 'Your parents thought that, I suppose? I'm not surprised. They clearly passed on their unruly faults to their whelp. Their stubbornness, too. Time to grow up, don't you think? You *will* move to the cemetery with the other badgers, and that'll be the end of it.'

Brockthorn rose onto his haunches and bared his fangs. 'And if I say no?'

'Then we'll destroy your home tomorrow morning' – the stag lowered his horned head and glared down at the badger – 'whether you're still inside or not.'

'How *dare* you,' Brockthorn bristled. 'My grandparents dug this sett themselves; my parents raised me from a cub. It's been my family's for ten seasons!'

'Your choice.' Rufus turned his towering frame

away from the badger and trotted away.

Brockthorn ground his teeth. He wouldn't be able to stop them; his teeth and claws might do some damage to one stag, perhaps even two, but no hope against a mass of jabbing antlers and sharp trampling hooves. The other woodlanders wouldn't risk helping either. This wasn't another petty disagreement about noise, or digging in the wrong place, and they all had their own homes and families to think of, anyway. They were getting tired of his constant arguments with Rufus and his herd. *Why pick a fight over every little argument? Just shut up for once and do what Rufus says. Relax and enjoy being safe.*

But how could he relax? Do what Rufus ordered or have his skull kicked in – not much of a choice. *Think for yourself* was what his parents had always taught him. But what else could he do? Leave? No mammal had left Richmond Park in countless seasons. Even the birds always came back after their winter migration. It just wasn't done.

Didn't mean he couldn't, though.

Enraged, Brockthorn roared after the stag's backside, 'I'd rather leave the park myself than stay here with *you!*'

Scat. Did I mean that?

Rufus sighed and turned to face him. 'Leave?

128

Really, Brock? You ever heard the phrase "cutting off your nose to spite your face"? Humans say it. It means you—'

'I *know* what it means,' Brockthorn spat.

'Very well,' Rufus continued. 'Look, *we're* in charge. Always have been and always will, that's just how it is here. But I'm not your enemy, Brock. This park's a wonderful haven where we can all live together in safety, where humans respect us and take care of us.' His voice hardened. 'But there *are* rules. Just follow the rules like everyone else and you can stay. The last thing we want is to drive anyone away. Be serious – do you really want to leave here and live out there among humans? Dodging their cars, being kept awake by their endless noise, grubbing their leftovers out of bins? Whatever would your father think?'

My father would never have put up with this.

'I'd rather eat their stinking scraps than prance around posing for attention like one of their pathetic pets!'

Rufus snorted and stomped a hoof. 'Watch your mouth, mud-muncher!'

Brockthorn smiled. 'You ever heard the phrase, "in for a penny, in for a pound"?' He raised his paws to his head like two extra large ears, and waggled his claws. 'Ooh, look at my big beautiful

129

antlers! Please, human, please notice me!'

Rufus reared onto his hindlegs as Brockthorn darted back. The deer's sharp black hooves smashed into the dirt, missing his hide by a whisker.

'I'll aim for your head next time,' Rufus bellowed, then cantered away through the trees. 'Like father like son!' The other badgers had witnessed the commotion and were frowning at Brockthorn.

Huh. *That* went well.

'Brock? Are you in there?' A soft voice echoed down the tunnel.

Brockthorn uncurled with a huff. Amber, the one vixen in the whole damn park that he did – and didn't – want to see right now. Above him, twisted tree roots snaked through the dry earthen ceiling.

'No,' he mumbled.

Amber padded down into the sett's main chamber where Brockthorn was curled up, nose buried in his flank. 'We were wondering if you'd changed your mind.'

Brockthorn snorted into his pillow of bristly fur. 'As soon as dawn breaks, Rufus will come with all his cronies and destroy my home. Hasn't left me much choice, has he?'

Amber nuzzled close and licked his cheek. 'Why're you being so stubborn? It doesn't have to be this way – come join us in the cemetery! They'll let you stay on if you just apologise.'

'No thanks.' Brockthorn buried his snout deeper into his flank.

Amber sighed. 'Now you're being ridiculous. There's loads of space there, more trees, and you can make a den twice the size of this one!' She brightened. 'Plus, the deer said we can hunt birds on the outskirts.'

Brockthorn glowered at her. 'Oh, the *deer* have said, have they? How generous of them! Do the *deer* tell you where to drop your scat as well?' he snarled.

Amber paled, then whispered, 'There's no need to talk like that. We're worried, too. As much as you hate Rufus's gang – and remember, you *know* I hate 'em too – you gotta admit that it's safe here, right? Rufus wants what's best for the park, and for everyone. He *may* be a real pain in the arse about it sometimes, but you have to see his point of view. The humans come to the park to see all us animals. We're like a show. As soon as you leave the safety of the park, you'll be just another annoying pest.'

'Open your eyes, Amber. The deer already treat us like pests. At least out there I'll be a pest who can do whatever he damn well wants. Nobody telling me what time to hunt, what I can and can't eat, when to be quiet, how big my sett can be . . . didn't Rufus mark you for bringing rats home once?'

Amber flinched, her muzzle drooping to conceal the half-faded scar crawling along her belly. 'That's . . . that's not the *point*.'

'And didn't Liam get a kicking for leaving fishbones out on the—'

She thrust her snout forwards. 'You're just exaggerating, like you always do. Liam's an otter – he knows the rules, same as anyone. Don't you understand that you could get squashed by a car out there, or mauled by a city dog?'

'I know. And I don't care.'

'How can you *not* care, Brock?'

'You don't understand. My grandparents built this sett when they first arrived here, my parents lived in it their whole lives, and now it's mine. Ten seasons.' Brockthorn uncurled and shook himself. 'Except it's not mine, is it? Never was mine, nor my parents', nor my grandparents'. As long as my sett's within this park, the deer own it. Like they own everything else. One deer suddenly decides he wants a new tree to scratch his backside on and – surprise, surprise! – we have to move.'

'We all make sacrifices, that's how it works here.'

'They're full of scat, Amber. Why can't you *see* that? All those excuses about their pond being too small, it's all lies. They just saw something they wanted and now they're taking it. Because they're bigger, stronger, and there's a whole herd of them.'

Amber frowned down at her paws. 'Maybe that's just the price we have to pay to live in safety here.'

Brockthorn scoffed. 'You think Richmond's the only park in London?'

'No. Of course not! But it's the biggest. The *safest*.'

'How d'you know that? Did those jumped-up twigheads tell you?'

Amber's yellow eyes widened. 'Because . . . it just *is*. Everyone knows that.'

Brockthorn began pacing the cramped hollow. 'My parents told me about the park my grandparents were born in. A big safe park just like this. Except more how it *used* to be, before Rufus. No one in charge telling anyone what to do. My father talked about going back there, before he died . . .'

'So why did your parents choose here, if this other park was *so* brilliant?'

'I dunno, they never said. Maybe my

grandparents never told them. But it was *normal* back then, wasn't it? You wanted a change of scenery, you just went somewhere else. Animals could come and go. Why stay in one place forever when you can explore? And Richmond Park used to be the same until Rufus became king of the herd. My mother said he changed everything, made all these new Park rules . . .'

'Fair enough, but you *know* what older generations are like . . . always yammering on about how great things used to be. Not all rules are bad, you know. They make us safe. Ensure there's enough food to go around. They stop all the city animals from trespassing too, don't forget. Do you really want to live somewhere where any old fox can come off the street and build their den right next to yours?'

'Ugh, you sound just like 'em.' Brockthorn slumped into the soil. 'I'm leaving, and that's that.'

'Look, can't I just—'

'Don't, Amber. There's no point.'

'Goodbye, Brock,' Amber whispered, 'I'll miss you.' She licked his cheek, then slunk back through the tunnel out into the cold night air.

'I'll miss you too,' Brockthorn murmured.

The loud tramping of hooves jolted him awake.

Brockthorn uncurled, gazed around his comfy familiar chamber and sighed. Shallow grooves from his grandparents' claws hung over him as they had for the last five seasons of his life.

And soon they'd be gone. Forever.

He trundled up the tunnel towards the blinding sunshine, the deer's booming voices growing louder.

'. . . he needs to go . . . enough's enough . . .'

'. . . don't know what he's playing at . . .'

'. . . won't last a day out on the streets . . .'

Brockthorn squinted up at the surrounding herd as he exited his only home for the last time. He forced a carefree smile, despite his knotted stomach. 'Calm down, lads. I'm out.'

Rufus loomed over him. 'You look cheery, considering. Finally decided to accept our terms, have you?' The other bucks lurked behind him, watching Brockthorn with narrowed eyes.

'Nope. Just happy to leave the lot o' you, to be honest.' The other woodlanders had gathered at the edge of the trees. Another strained goodbye with his friends was the last thing he wanted, but he couldn't let tears fall now. 'I'd best say goodbye to my mates then, before you crush my skull with your fat hoof, eh, Rufus?' As he trundled off, he heard Rufus snort.

'All right. Break it down.'

Head high, Brockthorn padded towards his friends as hooves and antlers began grinding into the earth behind him. His family home for ten long seasons, wiped out in a few agonising moments. *I made my bed, now I have to lie in it. There's another nice human saying for you, Rufus.* It took all his strength not to groan with grief.

'We'll miss you,' Corvus the raven croaked.

'You can still stay here.' Fern kneaded her bushy tail between her paws. 'Just come over to the cemetery with us.'

Their platitudes were sincere, but Brockthorn had always been a grumbling nuisance and they all knew it.

'Thanks, but I think I'll finally go find out where my grandparents came from. Besides, I don't think the deer want me around anymore.' He glanced back; Rufus's herd were busy destroying his home, collapsing the ceiling with their antlers and scraping loose earth into the chamber. Soon only a deep gouge in the churned earth remained, soil strewn all about. Brockthorn blinked, stemming the tears for a few more precious moments. He wouldn't give the herd the satisfaction of seeing him weep.

'Please just stay, Brocky,' Fern begged. 'You've

made your point.'

Brockthorn stared at the squirrel. 'Is *that* what you think, Fern? That I'd get turfed out, risk my life, everything my family built, just to prove a point?'

'That's not what I meant, I—'

'Save it.' Brockthorn turned away. 'Enjoy your new home, all of you. But I'm going.'

'Right you are!' a cheery voice piped up. 'And you ain't goin' alone!' Amber trotted up beside him, beaming.

Brockthorn gaped. 'Come with me? But it's far too dangerous. We'll be out in the cold and rain, dodging cars . . .'

Amber snorted. 'Sneaking through the big city? Pffft. That's what us foxes do best. Besides' – her voice softened – 'honestly, I've had enough of these stuffy old pricklers ordering folks around. Good chance to stretch my legs a bit, y'know?'

Brockthorn grimaced. 'It's far safer for you to stay here . . . I'm leaving, like it or not.'

Amber licked his cheek. 'Of course! And I'm comin' with you!'

Doubt gnawed Brockthorn's belly. 'Won't it be scary?'

The vixen shrugged. 'Sure. But we'll be less scared together. Which reminds me – Oi! Liam!'

she barked. 'Where you at?'

The otter bounded out of the shallows and shook himself dry, showering them with water.

'Ahoy there, matey. Heard you was thinkin' of a grand old adventure without me, eh? Not a chance!'

Brockthorn's stomach clenched. 'You too? Why risk yourselves for me? I'm just a grumpy old boar!'

'Yeah. Yer a stubborn old codger, but that's why we likes ya. And if anyone fancies messin' wid ya,' the otter bared a gleaming set of sharp white teeth, 'they'll have Liam Streampaw to reckon with.'

Brockthorn looked at Amber, who grinned back. 'I've got no other plans tonight. Lead the way.'

'Amber! Liam!' Rufus roared from the trees. 'Don't join this fool's errand! If you join that grumbling stripehead, you'll be banished from the park!'

'I'd rather take my chances with this grouchy old fleabag than cower under you stinking bullies any longer!' Amber yelled back. 'Good riddance to bad rubbish!'

'Friends, please!' Rufus pleaded as the three friends trotted away together. 'Don't go chasing a fool's dream. Isn't that the height of stupidity?'

Liam turned to smirk back at the stag. 'Depends, matey – how tall are you?'

14
CUNNING CANIDAE

'I'm starving!' Dusksilver whined.

Flamefur curled around her. 'It's okay, little one.' Frostbitten grass glittered about them like diamonds, as brittle and tasteless as sodden hay. Flamefur's stomach growled: only a harvest mouse since last night. Dusksilver nuzzled into her, shivering.

Hunger curled its claws into her belly; they couldn't go on like this, grubbing for worms in the frozen earth or gnawing the shrivelled berries from the hedgerows. Her cub needed meat. Tonight.

A piercing whistle sliced through the frozen silence, answered by a muffled bark. Flamefur's ears pricked – the farmhouse! Perfect.

They slunk down the icy lane to the garden, peering through the old wooden fence. The farmer was on his hands and knees cutting rows of frosted parsnips, his breath fogging the air. Two weasel corpses snarled down from the shed wall, their yellow fangs bared in death.

A vile stench of rotten eggs wafted over them. Dusksilver wrinkled her nose. 'Eww, Mum! What's that smell?'

Flamefur's eyes twinkled. 'Man's scat heap.' Beside the shed stood an open box of muddy boards, brimming with grass cuttings, mouldy vegetable peel and the sludge of wood-ash. Flamefur crept to the fence, Dusksilver close behind her as they watched the man pile the frozen vegetables into a wheelbarrow and cart them away to the kitchen door.

Dusksilver tilted her head in confusion. 'Why's he doing that?'

Flamefur narrowed her eyes. 'I suppose he wants to let them thaw tonight. Then he'll take them to market tomorrow.'

Dusksilver licked her chops. 'Yummy! Let's go, Mum!'

'Dusky, wait . . .'

Dusksilver wriggled under the fence. 'It's okay, Mum. There's nobody—'

A wild barking shattered the silence. The skittering of claws. Dusksilver scrabbled desperately at the fence. 'Help, Mum! HELP ME!' Flamefur wrenched her head through the gap and yanked Dusksilver back by her neck-scruff.

A black monster charged through the cabbage patch, spraying soil everywhere as he howled with excitement. Flamefur wheeled away with her safe cargo as the hound hurled himself at the fence, barking madly.

'That's it, Bear!' the farmer chortled. 'You chased them varmints off! Good boy!' Bear bounded around his legs, tail thumping as he panted with eagerness.

Flamefur lowered her wriggling babe in the safety of the wood. 'Dirty brute!' she snarled. 'He's trouble an' no mistake.' Her eyes softened as Dusksilver shrank against her, whimpering with fright. Flamefur nuzzled her close. 'Shhh. You're safe, Dusky. I'm here.' Her golden eyes gleamed. 'I dunno how we'll do it, but we'll eat his food inside the house and make that dog look a fat fool! You just watch!'

Tires squealed; a muffled thump close by. They trotted through the woods to peer into the lane. A great grey van fishtailed away from them, one rear door swinging wildly as it rounded the bend out of sight. A crumpled plastic bag lay in the middle of the muddy track. Dusksilver approached it warily, sniffing. Peering inside, she recoiled with a yelp of disgust.

'It's all rotten, mum! Yucky!'

Flamefur nosed inside and tugged out a string of raw sausages, the grey meat crawling with fat writhing maggots. Dusksilver slumped onto her paws with a mournful whine. 'It's no good, Mum! Useless!'

Flamefur's tail swished as she eyed the bag. 'Maybe not. C'mon. I've got an idea.' Mother and cub dragged the meat to the bottom of the vegetable garden and left it there.

Flamefur turned to her daughter. 'Remember that rubbish heap we saw?'

Dusksilver scowled. 'Yes.'

'How badly d'you want some grub?'

Dusksilver's stomach gurgled. '*Very.*'

Flamefur grinned. 'Now, you're not going to like this part . . .'

'Worse! Plan! Ever!' Dusksilver spluttered, spitting out a potato peel. Her fur was matted with mud, grass, and a month's worth of slimy vegetable waste. Beside her Flamefur squelched to the fence, ignoring her daughter's sullen mutterings.

'This ain't gonna work.'

'Sure it will. Come on!'

Bear shivered on the porch; his dog-flap was plugged up with an old cloth to keep out the chilly

142

frost. Suddenly Flamefur's warm lilting voice came drifting out of the night.

'O brave Bear! Are you there?'

Bear perked up and glared about him, bristling. 'Who's there? What d'ya want?'

'O faithful dog!' Flamefur murmured behind the fence. 'Most fearsome ratter, most blessed hunter Bear! Your rich reward is at hand! I bring great tidings!'

'Who're you?' Bear growled. 'No tricks now!'

'Tricks, Bear?' Flamefur sighed. 'Ah, I see you do not know me. But listen, faithful brave hound. I am the Magic Doggywoggy, servant of the mighty Sirius who dwells in the far Eastern sky. Look to the heavens, O brave ratter! Do you see his shining light?'

Bear squinted upward and, sure enough, there was Sirius bright in the evening sky. Flamefur's lilting voice continued, 'Your fame as a ratter has come to the ears of Star-Lord Sirius. We know your skill and cunning as the greatest ratter in the world. And thus I have been sent with great news. Come close to the fence, so I may know you better!'

She pushed her filthy nose through the crack as Bear padded closer, snuffling. Dusksilver held her breath, but the rotten stench safely smothered their scent.

'Noble rat-ripper,' her mother whispered, nudging Dusksilver to stifle her giggles, 'it is I, the Magic Doggywoggy, sent to honour you!' She smirked as Bear thumped his tail and slobbered with joy. 'Lord Sirius himself wishes to meet you. But there is a test, O brave boy. First you must be proven worthy. At the bottom of the garden there is a long rope of meat. Real juicy meat, for although we are mere fairy dogs we bring real gifts to noble brave hunters as yourself. Go now, find that meat and be not afraid; I will guard the house until your return. Trust me – Dusky, *stop sniggering!* – ahem. Trust me and your faith will be rewarded.'

Hunger gnawed at Bear's innards and the cold leached into his bones. Yet still he hesitated. 'But my master ordered me to guard the house . . .'

The cold smelly muzzle withdrew. 'Ah well,' Flamefur sighed. 'What a shame. I'm certain there's a dog in the next village who will surely—'

'No, no!' Bear pleaded. 'No, Fairy Doggywoggy, please don't leave! I trust you! I'll go at once! Only, please guard the house until I come back!'

Flamefur's warm soothing voice drifted around him. 'Fear not, noble hound. Only trust the word of great Lord Sirius. Go now, and prove your worth!'

Bear tore away into the darkness. Dusksilver perked up. '*Now* can we go in, Mum?'

144

Flamefur nipped her ear. 'What – and rob him of his trust? Certainly not, Dusky! We'll guard the house.'

They waited until Bear came trotting up to the fence, licking his lips and grinning.

'Well done, noble hound!' Flamefur murmured. 'The house is safe. I shall return to Star-Lord Sirius and tell him of your worthiness by trusting me. Now he wishes to return the favour.'

Bear sank onto his haunches, tail thumping the ground. 'Am I worthy? Am I a good boy?'

'Most certainly.' Dusksilver draped her paws over her snout to muffle her giggles. Flamefur nibbled her tail in warning. 'When the clock strikes eight Lord Sirius will be passing this way; he means to appear before you and honour your loyalty. Be ready, Bear, and await my return!'

They crept away into the night, silent as moon shadows. Dusksilver squirmed impatiently. 'Come *on*, Mum! I'm famished!'

Flamefur slumped onto her belly. 'Hush, Dusky. Just a little longer . . .'

Soon the distant church bells chimed the hour, eight slow echoes. They heard footsteps crunch on gravel as the farmer trudged out of the gate, heading for the warm welcoming light of the ale-house down the road. Once he had disappeared from view, mother and cub slunk back to the fence. Bear was pacing back and forth before the kitchen door, his breath steaming in the frosty air.

'The King is approaching, noble hound!' Flamefur whispered. 'With his three trusty captains Scat-Scoffer, Post-Pisser and Arse-Sniffer. Do you know the village crossroads?'

Bear whined with joy. 'Yes, yes! O let me show how loyal I am, dear Doggywoggy!'

'Very well,' Flamefur smiled. 'Go there and await the King. He has come far; do not fail him and great blessings will be yours!'

'Fail him?' Bear yipped. 'Never! I'm loyal, I'll prove it!' And he streaked away into the night.

'Quick!' Flamefur hissed. 'Sharpish now!' She and Dusksilver trotted to the kitchen door, tugged the cloth from the dog-flap and crept inside.

A glorious smell washed over them: the delicious scent of roasted meat. Dusksilver squealed with joy; on the tabletop lay a succulent roast chicken, its crispy honeyed skin glistening under the light. They dragged it into the larder and fell upon it eagerly.

'Good faithful hound,' Flamefur laughed through a mouthful of meat. 'How thankful he'll be to the King on his arrival. Imagine his gratitude! Have another chicken wing, Dusky.'

Alone at the crossroads, Bear waited eagerly in the frost. Eventually he heard footsteps crunching near. His master appeared out of the night; Bear whined in disappointment.

''Ullo, Bear!' his master frowned. 'What're you doin' here?'

Bear nosed about mournfully, his tail between his legs. His master watched him, puzzled until . . .

'Aw, good Bear,' he grinned. 'You came to meet me, didn't you? Good boy! C'mon then, we'll go home together.'

Bear hung his head in sorrow as the farmer clipped him to his leash and led him home.

The door handle rattled! Both foxes barely had enough time to slip behind a pile of sacks before the farmer came in, leading Bear by the collar. The hound was too dejected to smell the gnawed meat; he slumped by the fire while the man poured himself a cider. Suddenly he glanced down. The wind was moaning through the dog-flap.

'That damn door again!' As Flamefur watched in horror, he fetched a cloth and jammed the hole up tight. Then he drained his glass, scratched Bear behind the ear and trudged upstairs to bed, humming.

Bear lay by the fireside, gazing mournfully into the glowing embers. Flamefur padded behind a stack of baskets, safely hidden from view.

'O brave Bear!' she whispered.

Bear perked up, thumping his tail. 'Fairy Doggywoggy! Is that you?'

'It is, dear friend. I am so sorry for your disappointment, noble ratter. You didn't meet the King, did you?'

Bear sank his head onto his paws. 'No! He wasn't there.'

'Never mind,' Flamefur murmured. 'Don't be glum, Bear. I came personally to warn you of great danger ahead! My noble King is gravely ill! Luckily we are friends, otherwise your good master will be stricken with fever too.'

'Fever?' Bear whined. 'Oh no! How, good fairy?'

Thinking fast, Flamefur plunged on. 'Many good fairies and kind spirits there are in the star kingdoms of the Eastern night! Most are friends, but some – curse them! – are our deadly enemies. Worst of all is the hateful Goblin Rat; the curse of Hamlin, the Nutcracker's nemesis, the giant of Sumatra. He works by poison, cunning and disease, for he dare not openly fight our brave King. Even now his evil spies crawl through gutters and ditches, carrying deadly sickness – they ravaged this land many winters ago. But I came here to warn you, Bear! If this foul plague draws near – and the rats are closing in – it will slay both your master and mine. You alone can save him. I cannot.'

'Horrid vile demons!' Bear growled. 'I must do something! Please tell me, faithful Doggywoggy! Help me save him!'

'The rats spread their poison by spells and enchantments,' Flamefur continued. 'But if a real dog of flesh and blood were to run five times around this house, barking as loudly as he could, then the spell would be broken! Their cursed sickness would lose its power!' She let a wretched sob creep into her voice. 'But alas! You are shut in, Bear! I fear all is lost! Whatever can we do?'

'No, no!' Bear yelped. 'I'll save you, Fairy Doggywoggy, your mighty Star-Lord and my dear master too. Have faith! Here I go!'

His hackles bristled. His chest swelled. He bared his teeth and howled, loud enough to wake the dead. The windows rattled. Coals tumbled in the grate. The noise was deafening. Soon they heard thumping footsteps overhead. Yet still Bear barked, on and on.

''Ey, boy! What's the matter?' The man stamped into the kitchen, flung open the window and listened for burglars. But he heard nothing except the endless barking. Finally he scooped up his shotgun and trudged outside. Bear streaked after him and tore around the house, bellowing like a bull. The kitchen door yawned wide.

'Quick!' Flamefur hissed. 'Come on!' Mother and cub dashed into the garden and squeezed through the fence. They plunged into the stream and bounded out, gasping with delight as the muck poured off them. From behind came a wild yelping, mixed with angry cries of 'Shuddup! C'mere, damn you!'

'Noble hound,' Flamefur laughed. 'He's saved his master. Saved us all.'

'And given us free supper tonight!' Dusksilver danced around, giggling. 'Now let's go home!'

15
PAWS, CLAWS AND CONSENT

The sickly ewe had died overnight, a limp heap of damp wool huddled in the shade. Frost still jewelled the ploughed field as Karl and Jorak crept over the furrows towards their bounty. Before them the towering hedge was enamelled with blood-red rosehips and hard black sloes. Morning dew silvered the cobwebs hung over the shrubs. High above a raven hovered like a scrap of black cloth, saw his breakfast was lost and peeled away southwards with a mournful croak. All around lay the rich autumnal stench of rot, and both foxes tasted the dozen scents flavouring the dawn. Wordlessly they trotted close, lowered their heads and began feeding.

'You go first . . .'

'No, *you* ask him . . .'

'Ow, stop *pushing!*'

Karl lifted his bloody muzzle and looked around.

The whispering stopped. Seven male kits – five juveniles, two merely cubs – were all staring with wide startled eyes. Karl clenched his jaw; Ruki's newest litter. Perhaps he was just paranoid. Still a daunting new world for them among the skulk; it wasn't strange that their dark eyes followed him everywhere, or that they often stopped talking and lowered their eyes whenever he prowled by. Right? Not strange at all.

Except . . .

'What d'you want?' he asked. Beside him Jorak was still muzzle-deep in the ewe's belly, chewing away.

They mumbled and whispered among themselves, nibbling ears and nudging each other's flanks until the tallest finally edged forwards. He stood there, tongue-tied, shuffling from paw to paw.

'*What?*' Karl growled.

'Oh, um,' the kit shrank back, ears flattened. Karl thought his name was Thazi, but they'd never talked before. 'We were just wondering, uh . . .'

Another kit nipped Thazi's brush; he shut his mouth and hung his head, watching a beetle trundle past.

'Wondering,' a third kit – a lanky fluffball with crooked ears – mumbled, 'wondering if it's good when a lady screams?'

Karl must have had a murderous glare on his face, because they all cowered back, ears drooped. 'Why?' he demanded. 'What did you do to her?'

'Nothing! We didn't do nothing!'

The lanky one spoke up again. 'It's just, Rose, we uh, we hear her scream at night, and um, you—'

'Stop.' Karl growled in his sternest voice. The one that promised tears before bedtime if disobeyed. 'Cubs, *out*. Hey,' he turned to Jorak, 'you make sure they leave, and keep an eye on 'em, yeah?'

Jorak chuckled. 'Sure.' He twitched his brush and grinned as a cub pounced on the tag, then wrenched a bloody foreleg free, its hoof trailing behind. 'C'mon, cubs! Wanna play?'

The two youngest sulked and grumbled, but they soon scampered eagerly after Jorak, snapping and tugging at his bait as he led them away along the hedgerow. The five remaining kits huddled together, whispering and nudging.

'You *don't* talk about her that way.' Karl knew Rose didn't care whoever heard them at dusk, and he *loved* when she was loud, but there was a line. 'It's rude. You don't – you don't talk about *anyone* that way. You don't speculate about what two grown-ups do when they're alone together, okay? Ever.'

'But—'

'*Ever.*' Karl's voice was dangerously low.

'What's "speculate"?' asked a kit with white moulting patches on his hindquarters.

'Guess. Talk about. Gossip. It's *not* your business what other foxes do between themselves in private.'

One of the smaller ones was dabbing at his blood-speckled snout and looking embarrassed. 'But . . . she likes you, right? How did you get her to like you so much?'

By not treating her like an idiot, Karl didn't say.

'We just figured, I mean. She's your mate, so . . . you must be doing *something* right.'

Thazi asked, 'Where do you . . . ?' but trailed off.

More whispering, and shuffling, and gnawing of ears. Finally a skinny one Karl knew, Yann, crept forwards. 'Deran kissed a girl then asked her to play mates and she nipped him.'

The kit with the bloody nose scowled. 'Right inna face!' he whined.

'Well, *good*,' Karl muttered.

Deran pouted. 'Why's that good? She didn't have to *bite* me!'

'Did you *ask* before you touched her?'

Nobody answered, but all five looked confused. Karl sighed. 'You *have* to ask. You *always* have to ask before you touch anyone.'

154

'I asked!' Deran frowned. 'I did!'

Karl rolled his eyes. 'You don't ask like *that*. You don't just walk up to her then ask if she wants to play mates. You need to talk to her first.'

'We *do*, though!' the moulting kit started grouching. 'We talk to 'em and tell 'em why we're nice and brave and real clever and they never listen!'

'No, that's not . . . *no*.' Karl was not a tall fox, but he drew himself up to his full height, scowling.

Time to lay down some rules.

Some of his skulk-brothers barked, or growled, or snarled. Karl always found it far more effective to speak low and quietly, every word clear and precise as if to an idiot cub, bearing down with an icy glare. That way, the implied menace was unmistakeable. Calm words, patient voice, huge menacing posture. It had worked before, and was working wonders now. The kits huddled together, wide-eyed and swallowing hard and blinking in dumbstruck silence.

'You don't brag,' Karl told them. 'You don't boast, you don't try to impress girls. Right? That's *not* how it works.' His voice softened. 'You just . . . you just have to *listen* to them. Maybe give them nice compliments. Ask what their day was like. Did they catch anything interesting? Little things.

Maybe say they look good. Not just pretty.' He turned a stern eye upon Deran, who cringed low into the dirt. 'Girls are smart and fierce too, so make sure you tell them.'

Thazi piped up from the back, 'I said a girl looked like she ate really well and she ran away crying!'

Karl shook his head. 'Not like *that*, either. You just . . . you just talk. You have to get to know her first.' He winced as he said it, and winced more at their reactions.

'What?'

'Why?'

'How?'

'I ain't never talked to a girl since I was a cub with me mam!'

'We don't have to ask when it's just us!'

Karl ground his teeth. 'Right . . . *one*, whatever you've done between you is between you. But you have to *ask* girls first. Always ask.'

In reply he saw some frowns, and some hesitant nods, and plowed on.

'Two, you talk about other things first. You say hello. Tell her your name, and you ask for hers. And if she smiles back at you and doesn't chase you off, maybe you ask if she wants to sit by you at dinner.'

Thazi perked up. 'And at dinner you ask if she

'wants to . . . scream at night?'

'No, not—' Karl started, but now their curiosity had overridden their caution. They crowded forwards, jostling and yapping.

'What do you do when she says yes?'

'How d'you make her scream?'

'They have different between their legs, right?'

Ugh. Looked like he'd need to *sketch it out in the dirt*; today, Karl decided mournfully, was really not his day.

It was dusk when Karl shook off his solitude and slunk down to dinner. An old deer had been cornered down in Bluebell Grove and now Karl's belly groaned at the enticing scent. He halted above the wooded hollow, seeking out Rose, and his heart sang as she approached him. Clearly word had spread; all around the glade young tods were gazing at him with newfound respect, and the older silver-furred vixens smiled in approval. Kessa cackled with glee. Maya just winked, smirking.

He missed the open moor sometimes. Much more privacy in solitude. At least rabbits weren't tattletales.

When Rose came close enough to see just how uncomfortable he looked, her laugh turned into her fondest smile. 'You're a good fox, y'know.'

'*Please* don't make me do that again.'

'We'll find someone else, I promise.'

'I was thinking Tolam.' Tolam was a seasoned fighter who'd won a dozen mating squabbles, now with two full-grown daughters and a son. He was good at keeping his family safe, he treated vixens with due respect and reverence, and he could corral the older kits. 'Tolam would be a good choice.'

'I'll talk to him,' she smiled. 'Don't worry.' She trotted back to the crowded carcass and returned with a hunk of liver, placing it at his feet. 'Wanna find a quiet spot?'

When their bellies were full, and Karl had relaxed somewhat, Rose draped herself over him and began grooming, kneading his spine with both paws. Between blissful growls, he told her about the conversation.

She frowned. 'Not what I heard. They told everyone you said never to touch a vixen.'

'Mmm,' he grunted. 'If that's all they remember, 's fine with me.'

She nuzzled close and snuffled into his ear. 'But really you said they have to *want* it.'

'Mmm.'

'Both the tods *and* the vixens?'

'Mm-hmm.'

'That's . . .' she paused her grooming. 'Plenty of

foxes here who need that. Some of the older mates could learn, too.'

'Just leave me out of it.'

She chuckled and licked his cheek.

He rolled over, gazing up at her. 'Are you gonna teach 'em, then?'

She snorted, and he knew it meant no. Then she stilled, and leaned close to whisper, 'Thank you. Thank you for making it about' – she sighed, and now Karl heard tears in her cracked voice – 'about *yes.*'

He nipped a flea from her chestfur. 'That's what we're trying to do here, aren't we? Make this a better home?'

'Yes,' she murmured, snuggling into his warmth. 'We are.'

16
NEIGHBOURWOOD WATCH

Snowstripe smiled around at the bleary-eyed circle of woodlanders. 'Thank you all for coming so late. Now if I could call this meeting to order – Taunoc! Could somebody wake him up, please? Thanks. Now . . . you've all met our newest neighbour, I'm sure.'

A chorus of groans answered him. He raised his voice against the complaining. 'And I'll be sure to – *listen* – I'll hear from you all in due course, all right? Gavin, you go first.'

One of the squirrels stepped up, gnawing a claw and looking embarrassed.

'Happened again, boss. Vince this time, leavin' Nyreen's all smug like a rat who's nabbed the cheese! Then she sauntered out after with this big lazy grin on 'er face!'

The badger nodded to him. 'Thanks, Gavin. Tess, you've got something to share with us? Take your time, you're among friends here.'

One of the fieldmice shuffled forwards, kneading her tail between her paws.

'It . . . it was awful,' she sniffled. 'Normally you head outside at dimpsey, gather y'self some seeds an' berries an' then tuck the babes in fer the night. Nuffink's wrong, nuffink's the matter—'

'Last night, Tess,' Snowstripe prompted gently. 'What happened last night?'

Gavin handed her a dock leaf, and she blew her nose. 'It was horrible . . . screechin' and wailin' like some poor animal bein' torn to pieces! Dashed back to check on my liddle mites an' they was all crying their eyes out!' She gazed around the circle of mournful faces, her voice quavering. ''Tain't right, mates. Not with me newborns to bring up!'

Murmurs of sympathy arose around the gathering. Paws shuffled. Throats cleared. Snowstripe nodded gravely. 'Thank you, Tess. Well, mates, you know this has been going on for some time. Zack, the floor's all yours.'

A magpie hopped into the centre. 'Always the same, Snowy. That skulk o' foxes loiterin' down by the quarry, real bunch o' troublemakers.' He ruffled his feathers moodily. 'Those brushtails turn up at Nyreen's real late an' swagger straight inside like they owns the place. Never 'ave to announce themselves, not so much as a by-your-leave, nothin'! She never keeps 'em waitin', that's for sure!'

The fieldmice huddled together, whispering and nudging before one spoke up, 'I went around to ask Nyreen if she'd mind keeping the noise down and she drove me off! Got real snappy at me!'

Rocking her squirrelbabe to sleep, Hazel frowned. 'Perhaps we could have a word with the skulk instead? Tell them they aren't welcome lurking around here?'

The spokesmouse folded his arms and glared across the circle at her. 'Oh yes? And I s'pose we just pop down there all polite like an' ask 'em real nice?' He rolled his eyes. 'Announce ourselves and ask, "Ooh please sirs, d'you mind aaawfully just toddlin' off now, thankee kindly?" Ha!' He sat down again amid his tittering companions. 'You wanna volunteer, marm? 'Cause I sure ain't!'

Gavin wrapped an arm around Hazel's shoulders. 'You leave 'er alone! At least she's thinkin' how to fix this, instead o' lazin' about all day – found *you* nappin' under the hawthorn bushes, didn't I?'

Snowstripe rapped a claw against the tree trunk. 'That's *enough*, Gavin. I'm sure the rest of you have your own grievances against Nyreen? Let's hear them.' He gazed around, wincing as the

162

mutterings trickled in from all sides.

'Never pulls 'er own weight gettin' the winter stores in!'

'Lounges around every mornin' preenin' 'erself all pretty, while we've got young 'uns to feed!'

'Keeps us awake with her randy antics all night! We've got families here!'

'She lets those layabouts saunter around her patch, dribbling scats everywhere, foulin' all they see. Disgraceful!'

'It ain't proper, not for this quiet neighbourwood!'

Snowstripe held up a paw. 'This could go on all season. We ought to – you're asleep again, Taunoc!'

'Not me!' The owl jerked awake amid stifled giggles. He peered around, blinking slowly. 'Hmm, mm . . . did I miss much?'

'No, sir,' piped up another mouse, keeping a wary distance from Taunoc's talons. 'We're just talking about solving the problem. Of Nyreen keeping us all awake at night, sir.'

Taunoc blinked at the mouse, then around at the other woodlanders, his beak moving as he tried to work it out.

'Hmm . . . you're all talking?' he finally asked.

Gavin nodded. 'Yep.'

'So . . . so who's doing the *listening*?'

Snowstripe grimaced. 'We're getting round to that. Marshweb, any ideas?'

The old toad waddled forwards amid much eye-rolling and smirks; he loved the sound of his own voice. Gazing about with bulging milky eyes, he announced in a somewhat pompous croak, 'Friends, fellow woodlanders, it's clear that this newest neighbour of ours has been the cause of much grievance these past moons. I humbly suggest that, with this esteemed council's approval—'

'Oh, get *on* with it, ya chunnerin' windbag!'

After icily glaring about for the culprit (and several smothered sniggers from among the mice), the fat toad puffed himself up and declared firmly: 'Drive her out. Wait until her next suitor prowls by, then stand outside her den making all kinds of noise. That'll dampen their enthusiasm, for sure!'

Snowstripe nodded. 'Sounds like that might work. Let's have a show of paws – who'd like to give this a try?'

Every paw went up. The magpies and Taunoc each raised a wing. Snowstripe grinned around at them. 'All in favour. Good. Let's get going, then!'

The woodlanders crept through the forest, Hazel and Gavin leaping through the trees as the birds glided silently above them. The moonlight dappled the fallen leaves, and away in the east came the harsh yelps of rival foxes skirmishing in the quarry.

At the edge of a large clearing, Snowstripe raised a paw, and the others halted. Before them, Nyreen's den yawned between the roots of a broad oak. Gavin crept down beside Snowstripe, nodding at the bushes rustling across the clearing. 'Someone's coming!'

Out crept a young dog fox, ears pricked in anticipation as he sniffed the air. Snowstripe leaned over to Gavin and whispered: 'Jake!'

The young fox certainly knew where he was headed. Head high and nose twitching, he trotted straight towards the den, calling, 'Nyreen, you there? It's me, Jake! Still feeling frisky for tonight, darlin'?'

'Jake, come right in, my sweet!' Nyreen's husky voice answered. Smirking, Jake bent his head and padded into her tunnel.

Hazel scuttled down the tree trunk beside Snowstripe. 'What now, boss?'

The badger hunkered among the leaves and nodded towards the den. 'Now we wait . . .'

Suddenly a shrill wail drifted out of the darkness. It rose and fell again, punctuated by sharp yelps. The yowling tomcat screech echoed through the trees, fading away to a moan of ecstasy.

Gavin grimaced. 'If those two can fight as hard as they—' he whispered, but Hazel shushed him. The sounds grew louder once more, both voices melded in blissful passion.

Zack fluttered to the ground beside them. 'Just say the word, Snowy!' Both squirrels streaked back up the tree, awaiting the signal.

Raising his muzzle, Snowstripe roared, 'Now, everyone! Now!'

The squirrels shook the leafy boughs, rustling them loudly. Zack circled low over the den, chattering raucously. The mice scurried squeaking among the bushes. Taunoc alighted on a lower branch, beating his wings and screeching with glee.

Out both foxes tumbled, dishevelled and panting as Nyreen glared into the shadows. 'What in the seasons is that racket?' she snarled. 'I'm callin' the Watch on you!' Raising her muzzle she barked into the night, the woodlanders' titters echoing around her.

With a rumble of hooves Markus thundered onto the scene, a mighty stag with his crown of magnificent antlers. Towering grandly over the other woodlanders he gazed sternly about. The Woodland Watch had arrived; a respectful hush fell over the gathering, waiting for judgement to be pronounced.

Markus's dark eyes slid slowly around the clearing, gazing over the woodlanders clustered among the trees and the two foxes in a jumbled heap of tawny fur.

'Now now, what's all this, then?'

'I'll tell you what's going on!' Nyreen spat, advancing on the stag. 'Jake and I were getting nice an' cosy, minding our own business when *this* filthy stripedog' – she jabbed her muzzle at Snowstripe – 'brings all his cronies along to bother us! His gang need to be driven out, right now!'

Markus drew himself up to his full regal height and glared down at the vixen. 'Now just one minute, missie. Am I to understand that this –' his gaze drifted over Hazel and Tess, and his eyes twinkled, '– *gang* that you're accusing, includes these harmless young mothers, eh?'

'Who *cares* if they're harmless?' Nyreen screeched. 'They ambushed us and spoiled our evening, these filthy scoundrels!'

Markus stamped his hoof, and Nyreen cringed back. 'Now then, missie,' he rumbled, 'Insults ain't goin' to get us nowhere.' He swung his antlers towards Jake. 'And 'ow about you, young gent? Care to explain yourself, hm?'

Jake slunk forwards, grovelling on his belly. 'Please, yer 'onner,' he whined, 'we was only 'avin' some cosy time together. Didn't mean to disturb all these decent folks!'

Markus nodded. 'Well, now I've heard *your* side of the story.' He turned to the woodlanders. 'And what about all *these* folks? What's your complaints against Nyreen?'

Answers came rattling back like hailstones.

'Nyreen's disturbin' the peace!'

'Keepin' our young 'uns awake all night! Can't 'ave it go on!'

'Ain't proper for this neighbourwood!'

'She scared me half to death with all that screechin'! Most unladylike!'

Nyreen bared her teeth. 'No I never!' She nipped a flea from her belly-fur. 'Sometimes a girl just wants some fun after dark, y'know?'

Markus chuckled. 'Is that so, missie? Well, looks to me like you've been respectfully outvoted. You know I serve this community, and – dearie me – it *seems* as if most of these woodlanders don't want you around any longer.'

Gavin marched forwards. 'I buried six caches of nuts for wintertime, and someone's gone and dug most of 'em up already.' He scowled at the vixen. 'I bet it was her!'

'That's rubbish!' Nyreen sneered. 'You lyin' branchbounder, you've only buried four of 'em!'

A deathly silence fell. Markus slowly turned his horned head towards her. 'And how would you know that, missie,' he growled, 'unless you were *looking* for them?'

The fear that flashed across Nyreen's face was proof enough. 'I-I didn't . . . er . . .' She edged back, her eyes darting around a circle of stern frowns. She turned to flee, but Markus froze her in place with a glare of withering scorn.

'So that's what we're dealing with.' His voice dripped with contempt as he paced back and forth. 'Not only a noisy troublemaker, but a dirty common thief. Well, best you two rascals get goin' and leave these woodlanders alone. Don't want any more nighttime trouble, do you?'

Quaking with fright, both foxes cowered into the leaf litter. Markus jerked his head eastwards, towards the distant quarry. 'I save my horns and hooves for proper combat with true warriors – young bucks and brave veterans alike. Thievin' cowards like you would only dishonour their edge. But if either of you ever come skulkin' around these woods again, you'll get a taste of my fury soon enough. Remember, Markus Woodwatcher always keeps his word . . . now clear off, the pair of you!'

Humiliated, both foxes scrambled away into the darkness, their wails fading among the trees. The jubilant woodlanders crowded around Markus as he nodded to Snowstripe. 'Well, sir, best I be off. Thank you for bringing this fracas to my attention – glad those prowlin' nuisances were finally dealt with.'

Hazel hugged his leg. 'Thank you, sir!'

The noble stag bowed gallantly. 'Marm, 'twas a pleasure. G'night, all!' He strode away into the night, head held high as the woodlanders cheered him to the treetops.

Snowstripe gazed proudly around at them. 'Good work, mates! Now let's all get some shuteye. Hopefully there'll be no more of this beastly business . . . what? What's so funny? Why're you all laughing?'

17
LIFE OR LIMB

Church choirs had sung the harvest home across
Exmoor, from Challacombe to Dunster, Porlock and
Brushford. Basket offerings were laid at Old Man
Barley's feet, and the reddish-browns and burnished
golds of autumn had crept back over Snowdrop
Hollow where Fenbriar kennelled under the beech
trees, the Quarme river chuckling before him.

The young fox sniffed the air, sifting through the
dozen woodland scents that washed over him.
Collared doves erupted from the hazels and clapped
downriver, wheeling among the shafts of sunlight.
Cragmere the goshawk was waiting. He swooped
from the oak, corkscrewed over the glittering twist
of water and seized the slowest hen, scattering the
flock into the rowans. Cragmere flashed them an
arrogant glare before gliding upriver, the carcass
swinging limply from his talons. Deep within the
larch thicket a blackbird cried *chink chink!* and

ruffled its feathers. The Quarme was a thread of sunlight beneath the hazels. High overhead, chaffinches skirmished for roosting perches while dragonflies flitted along the riverbank. Chattering swifts circled the church tower of Exford, and across the southern fields the bus horn blared as it rumbled out of the village. White tufts of plumage littered the roots of the alder where Cragmere butchered his prize.

Fenbriar's nose twitched at the musky aroma of vixen; he smiled as Moonsmoke trotted out of the undergrowth. 'Hey, rosebud. Catch anything today?'

She snuffled into his ear before slumping alongside him with a weary huff. 'No luck yet. Found two conies snared down by Cragmill Cottage, but the trapper's only left their pads behind.'

Both foxes lifted their muzzles to taste the air. The trees bared their russet crowns to a rosy sunset; their bronze foliage shivered as unseen woodpigeons clattered and squabbled within. Moonsmoke yawned, then blushed as her stomach gurgled. Fenbriar chuckled and nuzzled her flank. 'Feeling peckish, dear?'

His mate giggled and gnawed his ear. 'Fine, *fine*. We'll get going in a minute – just a little higher,

172

please . . . aaahhhh, that's it!' She sighed in relief as Fenbriar showered her brow with tender licks, snuggling into his warmth as he groomed her.

Fenbriar's ears pricked as distant cawing sliced through the hushed stillness. 'Something's spooked the crows.'

'Yeah, I heard 'em too.' Moonsmoke raised her muzzle, sniffing the breeze. 'Greenlimb Wood, perhaps. Good hunting there, d'you reckon?'

'Let's find out. C'mon, then!' Fenbriar loped out of the trees onto the open moor, padding silently up the sheep path as Moonsmoke followed. The purple flowers of bell-heather shivered as bees gathered their golden harvest of pollen. Evening dew silvered the spiders' silk that veiled the gorse; both foxes dimpled the hoofprints of wild ponies as they skirted the western slope of Dunkery Beacon. High overhead, a skylark sang as it wheeled and dived. A party of rucksacked ramblers glimpsed them from the summit, but before any could focus their binoculars both foxes had vanished like wraiths into the rolling waves of purple heather.

Halfway down the hillside Fenbriar halted, sniffing the layered scents before him. Moonsmoke drew alongside, her head tilted quizzically. Fenbriar pointed his muzzle towards a rustling patch of bracken and whispered, 'Good old Ashgar!'

Moonsmoke grinned as a twig snapped. The bracken quivered before them; whoever it was had no ear for stealth whatsoever. Moonsmoke leaned against her mate, shaking with silent laughter. Fenbriar smirked and crept forwards, eyes fixed on the white-tipped brush protruding from the bush.

He pounced.

'Yowch!' A tawny head dusted with silver burst above the scrub, scowling. The heather rippled as chittering conies streaked away through the bushes.

The old fox watched them escape, then rounded on Fenbriar. 'Cheeky young scamp! What d'you do *that* for, eh?'

'Made enough noise yet, grey-muzzle?'

Ashgar snorted. 'What gave me away?'

'Sly old dog,' Moonsmoke giggled, 'you're loud enough to frighten off all the conies this side of Dunster! Always stay low when you prowl, remember? You taught us that only last winter!'

'Hmph! Getting clumsy in me twilight years!' Ashgar rolled onto his back, baring his throat in deference.

'Get up, old grandfather,' Fenbriar smiled, nudging Ashgar back onto his feet. 'Any luck this morning?'

Ashgar hung his head. 'Lost a rat to Shiv the stoat at daybreak.'

'Did you?'

'Then got sniffed out by the farm hounds down at Winsford Mire.'

'Oh dear. That sounds—'

'You ever lain low in a muddy bog for over three hours under the baking sun, waiting for a beagle bitch to quit sniffing around?'

'Well, *no*, but—'

'Yeah. That happened. *Then –*'

'Oh, *seasons*,' muttered Moonsmoke. Fenbriar smirked and nudged her as Ashgar continued grouching: '– *then* a fat white hen decides to kick up a ruckus down at Hazelberry and the terrier chases me off. And then, *right* when I've got a nice bumbling coney within easy reach, you decide to play pounce-the-mouse! Ugh. So yeah, not a great day. However,' he added, brightening, 'we haven't had a thunderstorm recently.'

'Indeed we haven't,' Fenbriar agreed weakly.

Ashgar shrugged. 'Other than that, can't complain, really.'

Moonsmoke bit the tag of her brush to stifle a giggle. 'Where will you roam tonight, wise sage?'

Ashgar licked a paw and washed his gaunt face. 'Agh – still feel a bit stiff. That beech grove over yonder looks promising.'

'Watch your step round there,' Fenbriar warned

him. 'The trapper's left snares down by Cragmill in Bramble Wood. Stay safe – his dog's out loose again.'

Ashgar shuddered. 'I'd rather have a pack of bloodhounds breathing up my arse than that black brute trailing me. He never loses a scent. Never!' He squinted up into the gathering dusk. 'I'll probably kennel up by Sharptooth Rocks tonight. Sing to the stars. To Elmora.'

Moonsmoke licked his cheek. 'Put in a good word for us, won't you? Tell that old brushtail we all miss her.'

The old fox nibbled her ear fondly. 'I always do. Run with your head high, little sister.'

They left Ashgar and ran downhill through the gorse. A pheasant whirred up from the scrub and its harsh scolding pursued them over the Exford-Luccombe road. Side by side they trotted through twilight down into the wooded valley, the Horner stream tumbling over lichened boulders before them. Twisted oaks snaked together, their gnarled limbs choked with moss while leaf mulch clogged the roots.

Moonsmoke streaked ahead with an eager yip through the lengthening shadows, her nose twitching as she singled out a thread of coney scent. 'C'mon, slowworm! Don't dawdle!'

Fenbriar hesitated amid the rotting leaves. The heavy silence prickled his hackles, for no woodpigeons crooned. No songbirds trilled.

Quiet. Far too quiet.

The damp earthy odour of moss, dead leaves and pony dung drifted over him, spiced with the enticing scent of mouldering rabbit. Suddenly the rank stench of the trapper set his senses quivering and the gin-metal taint soured the air; a hideous surge of fear froze his limbs like ice-water.

'Moonsmoke!' he barked, scrambling after her through the undergrowth. 'Moonsmoke, don't touch anything!'

'What d'you mean, silly?' she laughed. 'Over here – there's a dead coney!'

The trap clanged shut.

And Moonsmoke screamed.

Fenbriar burst into the clearing, his guts knotted with dread.

Moonsmoke writhed upon the ground, screeching and wailing amid bloody leaves. The gin's iron jaws had crunched deep into her left hindpaw and she thrashed helplessly, wide-eyed with agony.

Fenbriar dodged a flailing swipe. 'Please stay still, my love,' he pleaded. 'I can't help if you don't stay still!' He hunkered down alongside her, struggling to keep his voice low and steady. 'Trust me: you need to *relax*. If you don't, it'll only kill you faster—'

He flinched back as Moonsmoke snapped at his nose, missing by a whisker. 'Kill me faster?!' she spat. 'Great – *now* I can relax!' The acrid stink of terror rose from her coat as her eyes flooded with bitterness. 'Agh! Get it off me! Now now now!'

Fenbriar gnawed frantically at the metal chain with his fangs. 'I'm trying!' No good. His grip jolted loose again and he yelped in dismay.

'What can you do?' Moonsmoke sobbed. 'I ain't hobbling around with this on my leg.' She bared her throat and rasped, 'Well, finish it – kill me!'

'*Never!*' Fenbriar pressed his brow against the vixen's, her pitiful whimpers shaking him to the bone. 'Wherever you go, I go. We run together, love together, feed together and stay together. Forever and always.' Moonsmoke licked his cheek, gazing miserably into his eyes.

'Whatever can we do?' he whined.

'You already know,' a calm voice answered him. Ashgar's muzzle appeared through the birch thicket, eyes bleak with sorrow. 'Save her life. Do what must be done.' He gently licked Moonsmoke's mangled hindpaw, then met Fenbriar's gaze.

Fenbriar gaped at him, horrified. 'I . . . I can't!'

'You *must*. It's the only way she'll live to see the dawn.'

'But she'll be crippled! A three-legged vixen—'

'– can still birth cubs and live to be old and grey,' Ashgar grimaced. 'Some three-legs have even reached my sunset years. Far better to be a live cripple than a proud corpse.' He nodded at Fenbriar. 'Do it quickly; the trapper will soon return.'

Moonsmoke wriggled feebly. 'You'll get tired of nursing a useless cripple,' she sighed to Fenbriar. 'What good will I be? I couldn't chop a sleeping frog on three legs – I'm better off dead!'

Fenbriar pressed himself against her, his thick fur soothing her quaking limbs. 'Don't talk rot!' he growled fiercely. 'You're mine as I'm yours, remember?' Tenderly he licked Moonsmoke's muzzle. 'Does it hurt, my love?'

She clenched her jaw. 'No. It still aches, but . . . there's hardly any pain now.' She nuzzled her snout beneath his chin. 'Please get it over with, quickly!'

'Look into my eyes, Moonsmoke,' whispered Ashgar. 'Forget everything else, and listen to me.' Her head slumped onto her forelegs, eyes drifting shut as his soft deep voice bore her away across a calm quiet sea of aching memory. He sang of the vigils at the vole runs under warm summer evenings, the waves whispering against the northern cliffs, and of the fieldmice in the wheat under the cool moonlight. He sang of winter's chill caress, of the redwings guzzling the hawthorn berries and of the star-kissed fields of the Hereafter carpeted with endless rabbits. He sang of Rhaza the golden fox who rose from the hills each dawn to breathe life onto the land, and of Vishka his silver-furred mate who bounded across the sky every night, dancing among the stars.

Moonsmoke drifted through the sweet memories of her half-forgotten cubhood – and there she was! Lying in dry leaves in a sandy den among the warm wriggling bodies of her mewling brothers and sisters, and her mother was sliding her long belly over her, and Moonsmoke was reaching up to suckle . . . She nuzzled her head against Ashgar's and whimpered aloud.

'Shhh,' Ashgar comforted her. 'There, there, sweet cub. You're the bravest girl I know.' The vixen closed her eyes. Her body had drifted away, and numbness sank down into blissful peace – was death like this? Afloat on a gentle sea of the past off into the endless night? Ashgar's soothing voice washed over her like gentle summer rain.

'All animals die,' he chanted. 'Men and beast, fish and fowl alike, even the hounds that chase us will grow old and wither away. The seasons turn ever onward, seas rise and mountains fall – even the stars will burn out someday. And if we die, we die. But first . . . we'll *live*.'

A blinding jolt of pain, sharp and sudden. She gasped with shock, looked down . . .

. . . and breathed out.

'It's done,' Fenbriar murmured. He and Ashgar gently licked away at her maimed leg until the raw wound was clean and the bleeding had stopped. They helped Moonsmoke upright onto shaky paws, supporting her quivering body between themselves.

Moonsmoke limped forwards on trembling legs. 'I can't hobble around like this for the rest of my life,' she whimpered. 'I can't! It's hopeless!'

Ashgar licked her brow. 'Everything heals with time. You'll get used to it. Fenbriar will care for you, and I hope you don't mind getting fussed over by a long-toothed old dog either! Don't give up now.'

She clenched her teeth and nodded, her resolve firming like ice. She would not cower and whine like a frightened cub any longer. She was better than that. Far stronger than that.

They took her up the river valley deeper into Horner Wood, the trees whispering above them. A blackbird chittered from the upper boughs of a gnarled hornbeam as they padded through the undergrowth. Finally they reached the crumbling walls of a long-abandoned cottage, Ashgar nosing ahead among the ruins.

Moonsmoke sagged against her mate, panting. 'I'm useless like this – even slower than a blind old mouse!'

'Still much quicker than me, then!' Ashgar raised his head from a nearby bolthole, grinning. 'Down here's perfect for kennelling. There's two more boltholes out back, hidden by bushes. The den's big enough to raise a dozen cubs, and the ferns and broken timbers hide it real well. Warm and dry, solid stone walls too – no man could ever dig you out.'

Doubt gnawed Moonsmoke's guts, for the foul stink of man still clung to the mossy stones, tainting the air. 'I don't know . . .'

Fenbriar licked her cheek. 'It's the safest shelter for now. Once the oaks are in full leaf again by summer you'll be invisible – not even a buzzard would know anyone's kennelling here.'

They laid Moonsmoke to rest in the earthen hollow deep beneath rotten floorboards. Ashgar lifted his muzzle to taste the night. 'There's plenty of rich pickings nearby – farmyard chickens, grazing sheep and fieldmice nests. More coney warrens across the valley there. You won't starve, that's for sure. We'll look after you.'

Moonsmoke blushed. 'No need to trouble yourself further. Not for me.'

Ashgar bowed his head gallantly. 'Least I can do. Perhaps I could provide the odd rat or dumb coney, if milady would accept such gifts from a ragged old fleabag?'

She smiled and nodded. Ashgar padded to the entrance, calling back dryly, 'Besides, the sorry state I'm in, you'll probably need to start nursing *me* soon!'

He trotted into the wood, their laughter echoing in his ears. Then Moonsmoke's wound twinged; she flinched and hissed through her teeth. Fenbriar curled up beside her and snuggled close, licking her stump.

'I'm still such a helpless burden,' she muttered. 'Can't catch anything myself, can't even stalk a legless mouse now!' She heaved a long shuddering sigh. 'You'll leave me eventually, court another vixen—'

Fenbriar chomped down on his grief and silenced her worries with gentle licks. 'I'll never abandon you,' he whispered. '*Never*. My spirit is yours, my heart is yours, together as one. Besides . . . tomorrow is another day. And we'll face it together.

Just like always.'

'Now and forever.' Moonsmoke smiled and nuzzled into his tender embrace on the star-speckled leaves, letting blissful sleep wash everything else away. High amid the moon-silvered branches of Horner Wood, the nightjars were singing.

About the Author

Half-Welsh, half-Brummie, and terrible at both accents, Tom Burton has lived in Nigeria, Oman and the Netherlands. He currently lives with his family in Devon, his writing fuelled by the magic of dark chocolate and Yorkshire Tea. His short stories have featured in numerous online journals including *Spillwords Press*, *Literally Stories*, *Dreaming in Fiction* and *Whatever Keeps the Lights On*. *Wildlands* is his first published collection of short stories.

Printed in Great Britain
by Amazon